GURU IN THE GLASS

A MYSTERIOUS ENCOUNTER WHILE DYING TO LIVE THE UNLIVED LIFE

By

CURTIS TYRONE JONES

PLEASE ENJOY!

D.J.

First Printing: June, 2019

Cover Design by Angie Alaya

www.fiverr.com/pro_ebookcovers.com

Book Design by Will Silva

www.fiverr.com/tlmason

Edited by Josh Heath

joshua13heath@gmail.com

TABLE OF CONTENTS

GURU IN THE GLASS

"The world is more magical, less predictable, more autonomous, less controllable, more varied, less simple, more infinite, less knowable, more wonderfully troubling than we could have imagined being able to tolerate when we were young." ~ James Hollis[1]

"Dear wanderer, come in and let the weight of the world's straps slide from the downcast face of your unhappy shoulders, because the universe is a bartender and life is a perpetual party where all the drunken birds join with songs to sing the anthem of your beautiful existence." ~ Curtis Tyrone Jones

1 VOICES OF DESPAIR

Not long ago, there was a man named Skyler Deavensby who, after years of internal debate, determined that he was going to end his life. Maybe Thoreau's quote was true that *"Most people lived lives of quiet desperation,"*[2] but there was nothing quiet about the voices of despair that plagued Skyler's thoughts. He just couldn't figure out how life came so easily to others while it was so skilled at slipping through his fingers. The position that Skyler resigned from that day was the single greatest blow to his confidence. At one point, the job had been a magical step up to worthwhile work when he needed it most. But it had quickly lost its flavor and he had spiraled into an irresistible cycle of self-sabotage just like all the other positions that he had once loved.

Walking out of the building that evening, the feeling of excitement that Skyler normally felt upon quitting a job was now absent, non-existent, extinct. It was this lack of feeling by which he knew that he no longer had any drive to believe that there was a life out there that could satisfy his deepest longing for connection, creativity and adventure. As Skyler sat in his car at the top floor of the employee parking structure contemplating what he had just done, he took one last look at his life insurance policy that guaranteed that his family would be financially covered in the aftermath of his death. What he didn't realize however was that there was a clause in his policy that read, "The terms of this policy will be null and void in any and all cases of suicide."

After he had "verified" his policy, he turned the key to the ignition and started the car. The last chapter of his latest audiobook began to play over the speakers and Skyler realized with a pang of regret that this would be the last book that he would ever listen to. Through his years of internal agony, books had been his constant companions and his drug of choice, helping him to breathe a little easier when the elephants sat on his chest, and they numbed some of the pain when the thoughts began pounding at his mind with their relentless jackhammers.

There was never a time when Skyler wasn't reading some classic literature or listening to some latest installment in a new epic series. His wife Tulip joked that if the house was on fire and Skyler had to choose between saving his books and saving her and their four kids, she had a good idea of what decision Skyler would make. Skyler thought that her joke was just that, the root of her sarcasm was ungrounded and he always reassured Tulip that she and the kids were his most prized possessions. But Skyler always came away from those conversations sullen and more somber just from merely thinking hypothetically for a few moments about living without his books.

Checking his watch, Skyler determined that the occasion could afford and even deserved one last parting word, so he sat there and heard the final minutes of his book as a dead man at a wake silently hears the voices of his most trusted friends before being lowered into the earth. The story that Skyler had been listening to for the past few days, had been a dismal and dreary account of a woman named Amalie who had been abandoned by her parents as a little girl, abused by her guardians as a teen, unjustly treated by society as a young adult and battered by her lovers in adulthood. Even with all of this, the constant theme of

Amalie's resilience that was repeatedly threaded throughout the narrative was that, "She felt deflowered by life, but she refused to feel dethroned."

In a strange way Skyler envied Amalie, not because of her suffering but because of the indomitable personality that enduring her suffering had built in Amalie. Even in the midst of heartache she had a feisty character that only seemed to intensify in her agonies rather than diminishing. The grim anxiety and melancholy that Amalie faced was familiar to Skyler, but he couldn't help noting how they each came to their shared mental anguish through some very stark differences.

Amalie's life had been repeatedly ransacked and demoralized by people who were bigger and stronger than her. But the despair that Skyler had suffered had not involved one trace of injustice. Not only had people *not* been particularly unjust towards Skyler, but he couldn't even say that life itself had been unjust towards him. There had been no untimely deaths amongst his loved ones. Skyler had not been cheated on romantically, much less abused. He hadn't even been walked out on by true love. On the contrary, his wife Tulip was his best friend, and although their relationship could use some work from time to time, it had always been genuine and loving.

Skyler felt that his depression was an embarrassment in comparison to Amalie's. This woman was a hero in his eyes, not because she was winning at life, far from it, but because she had been knocked senseless time and time again and refused to give in. Skyler, on the other hand, had never even faced what he considered to be any formidable trials, and the people in his life generally liked him. Yet still, here he was, ready to quit everything in sharp deviation from the protagonist of his final novel.

"Maybe my depression doesn't even deserve to be categorized as depression," Skyler thought to himself.

Nevertheless, he couldn't deny that no matter what name you gave it, the effects of his mental deficiency was just as real and just as debilitating as anyone who "deserved" the diagnosis. It had been a silent killer crippling his confidence, maiming his ambitions and leaving his dreams for dead even though (and this was the worst part) Skyler himself had never faced any visible adversities in life.

There's an old urban legend that described the root of Skyler's misery in a nutshell. It says something to the effect of this . . . "In speaking to his class one day, a college professor quoted Socrates as saying, 'The unexamined life is not worth living.' Hearing this, a brilliantly witty and perceptive student raised his hand and shot back saying, 'Yes, professor, but the unlived life is not worth examining.'"[3] Contrary to Socrates' words Skyler had no problem examining his life over and over again to the point of analysis-paralysis. But unfortunately, even though he had mastered the philosopher's advice, Skyler had still found that his life was not "worth living" without any plausible reasons why.

But this simple depiction of the "unlived life" voiced in the young student's rebuttal pinpointed the source of Skyler Deavensby's devastating downfall. His whole life had been lived inside of other people's books and stories, but Skyler lamented that he had no story of his own. Other people, something deep within himself and even those damn reoccurring dreams, had always validated that Skyler had so much to offer. But if someone had asked Skyler what it was that he had to offer or even how he intended to offer it, he would have been clueless. Some people escape from their inability to live their unlived life by wreaking havoc on others. Skyler escaped from his ability to create his unlived life by mentally wreaking havoc on himself. As strange as it may sound, his relationship to this mysterious unlived life was the formidable enemy that had been invading Skyler's thoughts and silently punishing him for years.

What bugged Skyler about Amalie's story was that unlike himself, though tragic and wrought with mistakes, Amalie's life had been worth the read or "worth examining" because she had lived it with everything she had. Amalie's life may have been getting stomped by life's proverbial bull, but she was still "in the arena" rather than spectating from the sidelines or high up in the stands where one "neither knows victory nor defeat," to paraphrase Teddy Roosevelt's famous "daring greatly" quote. But tucked away in the safety of the stands as an onlooker or a fly on the wall was always precisely where one could expect to find Skyler Deavensby; never without a book in hand or playing through his headphones, of course. As Skyler sat there in his car making these distinctions, the story came to a close with this unexpected and infuriating line that somehow seemed to push the right buttons to unearth another side of him. Speaking of Amalie in a voice that signaled finality, the narrator concluded . . .

> *Standing cold on the precipice of an old bridge, deciding whether to live or just exist, she exhaled the plume of a deep breath and dropped a match incinerating the path to her past as the wings of her future burst from the blades in her back and flapped to new lands and new loves at last.*

In an instant, everything that Skyler had adored and admired about Amalie was stripped away from him and he sat there seething with what was for him uncharacteristic anger. Skyler's first thought was "Why can't life be this easy?" But since voicing any notion of jealousy concerning Amalie's end was a feeling that hurt worse than being kicked in his manhood, Skyler fended off the attack by shoving the feeling back down almost as quickly as it arose. Instead, he twisted his face in annoyance and scoffed,

"Finally a book that has the decency to give us a straight shot of the inconsolable nature of life and it ends by watering down its epic realism with a chaser of impossible fantasy?" For the first time Skyler was able to name a secret vendetta about many of his books that had always snagged on his own personal experience, but which was just now causing him to unravel.

"No one gets wings in the real world and some people never actually find happiness in the end," he murmured to himself.

Unhinged, Skyler ripped his iPod and the listening library it carried from its jack and hurled it out of the car window as his tires peeled and he sped off down the parking structure exit ramp on his way home. Leaving Skyler's hand, the iPod was launched off of the side of the parking structure and sailed its course going the way of gravity until it smacked solidly into the pavement below, immediately cracking open and exposing the entrails of its electrical wiring and its delicate programming.

That night, Skyler determined that he was going to jump off of Everest Bridge and be done with it all. The height of Everest Bridge made certain that Skyler would achieve his goal. Historically it had come to be named Suicide Bridge for completing the task of which so many sojourners of every age, economic status and educational background had come to this small town seeking out its services. It's quite possible that Skyler chose death by way of a bridge in strict defiance of Amalie's story, her wings and as a way of making a statement not only to Amalie of course, but also to his many books and to the whole universe of fictitiously optimistic endings.

After heading home and putting all of his affairs in order, Skyler wrote a goodbye letter to Tulip and the kids. In it, he wanted to conceal his underlying vexation towards his books so that he could still clearly convey his feelings about what was most

Pressing his eyelids together for what seemed like hours, he finally opened them to find that he was faced to face with himself in the reflection of the puddle. In that moment, though it was all mere seconds, he envied the mythical Narcissus and any other mystical creatures that could actually love what they saw in their mirrored reflections. He despised his and compulsively roared at the top of his lungs in disgust, "I hate you!" The onlookers thought that Skyler was speaking to the man with the dogs, the driver of the bus or maybe even life in general. No one suspected that it was the very same man peering back from the other side of the puddle, which was the aim of all of Skyler's bitterness and wrath.

A businessman in a clean suit and equally expensive shoes and a curly haired girl who appeared to be a college student heading to night classes who'd just dropped her books, both stepped down into the water to help Skyler up. But he pushed these two away, grumbling something about not needing any pity from people since no one really cared anyway. Drenched in shameful despair, he hobbled on from there, dried off somewhat and lost himself in a bar. There he passed out for a few hours, all alone, facedown on the table with his arms dangling below it before awakening and continuing on his way.

He did not awake first however, before the events of the day swirled around his head, taunting him as they always did with the dream that he always had each night that he would quit a job. He knew that this dream was coming. He also knew that in the same way that his dream job had become a nightmare to him, this dream, which once uplifted and infused him with possibility would also now just be a source of pain and confusion: A dreaded swift kick to the ribs while he was down. Even more than avoiding his family, avoiding the dream is why Skyler wasted no time in preparing his travel plans to make it to the bridge. He was hoping to outwit the dream and beat it to the punch before rest had a chance to find him and overtake him that evening. But his dream had proven once again, to be cleverer and more persistent than he was.

 AN UNEX-PECTED ENCOUNTER

It was late now, and all of the shops were closed having completely shut down for the evening. As Skyler walked to his destination, he was painfully aware of being sandwiched by his shadow on his right and the reflection of himself in the store windows on his left. For some unexplainable reason, these two companions reminded Skyler of the two strangers that tried to help him up out of the puddle earlier that day. Since he couldn't push his shadow and his reflection away as easily as he'd shoved the others, Skyler lashed out at his shadow belligerently yelling, "Hey! Are you here to help me up out of the water too? Let's see if you can help pick me up out of that river once that bridge has its way with me!"

As if his shadow felt the thrust of his words as solidly as the businessman felt the force of Skyler's hands that evening, his shadow magically receded into the night as he continued to walk. Relieved and satisfied by this sudden and unexpected response from his shadow, Skyler felt quite certain that he was responsible for sending his shadow away and not that it was his position as it related to the angles of light from the lampposts. Feeling empowered now, he turned to his reflection in the window to create more mischief with it and further test his new powers of sorcery. But before he could even get the words out of his mouth, Skyler was immediately startled as he yelled loudly, stumbled and shuffled backwards from the window on palms and feet, never taking his eyes off of what he'd seen through the glass while trying to escape it.

Walking from one side of the store to the next just like Skyler's reflection would have been walking and mirroring his exact stride, pace and facial expressions there was a woman walking in time with his footsteps. The woman, who'd now become his reflection, had even turned her head with an exact synchronicity of the movement of Skyler's neck and looked him directly in the eyes as his reflection would have, had he been looking at his own reflection. He *had* been looking at *his own* reflection, only now his reflection in the window was not himself, but it was a woman standing there as clear, captivating and as inescapable as the moon on a cloudless night. Although she had mirrored all of his initial movements, she had not stumbled back from the window in fear as he had done. But now she stood there sturdy and resolute, peering down at Skyler rather inquisitively.

At first, through absolute fear and since she was still fresh on his mind after pushing his shadow away, Skyler thought that what he saw was a phantom of the young college student who'd been with the businessman and whom he'd also shoved away earlier that day. Even though the silhouette of their hair and their height was an identical match, he immediately rejected the thought because this woman in the window, although strikingly beautiful, was clearly twenty to thirty years older than the girl. However, although she was not dressed to impress, *"Unless it's the beer goggles,"* he thought, everything about her was gorgeous and brilliant. Her eyes held a soft luminosity and exotic mixture of silver, blue or greenish depending on how the light touched them.

Skyler was struck by unmistakable tones of confidence and bravery in the depths of her utterly relaxed eyes. It was as if he wasn't a man but simply a mouse that had just mistakenly stumbled out of the bushes into a circle of lions and now found itself peering into the face of a calm lioness at rest amongst her pride who was unable to be troubled or checked by the feeling of any immediate threat. Skyler found himself lost in her domain, not even daring to move another inch or even breathe another breath for fear of startling it and transforming this motherly creature into something else that he was quite certain she was capable of becoming.

Her eyes held an intensity that he had never in his life experienced before. But those same eyes were so comfortable that clearly, even though Skyler was significantly larger and stronger than her, especially with his liquid courage from the bar, he was still no cause for alarm in her eyes. This was her territory and he had been reduced from a grown man to mere child's play in her presence. He felt certain that the tension in the gaze between them was so solid, like a string that was strung so tight, and it was so electric that Skyler swore he could have made that string sing like the musical mastery of Carlos Santana with a simple pluck of the energy between them.

The woman's hair was long and alive with a crown of untamed highlighted chestnut curls, which continued to dance with charm to the beat of their own rhythm for a few moments even after the woman's movements had ceased. Her skin was a smooth mysterious olive tone that appeared golden at times. On the woman's right arm was a tattooed sleeve of intricate tribal symbols from various cultural backgrounds that wove themselves around the woman's wrist and forearm to her lower bicep in the coiling body of an ominous snake. As sinister as this sleeve of serpentine symbols was, perched upon the neck of this fang baring cobra was an owl whose talons clutched at its prey with an unforgiving grip and whose eyes were just as intently focused on Skyler as the woman was. The owl completed the bicep and triceps portions of the artistry up to the shoulder. But ultimately, perched atop this artistic masterpiece of a mural and upon the owl was a tilted yet royal crown studded with valuable gems and diamonds of many shapes and sizes.

On her left arm was the full sleeve of a silver and black striped tiger that climbed the length of the woman's arm and looked back at Skyler with menace in the bared daggers of its mouth and equal amounts of treachery in its implacable and merciless icy blue eyes. It was obvious that some mixture of floral ink designs cut through the woman's sleeveless dress. These adorned the smooth skin of her lower neck and the upper area of her chest where the design connected one shoulder to the other.

But the rest of her advancing botanical and blossoming arrangements, as well as where they may have ended, were left to the imagination as her bohemian styled dress covered her all the way down to the thongs of her sandals. These braided themselves along the high arch of her instep and entangled themselves around her ankles in well woven anklets, revealing elegant feet whose toes were simply polished in what seemed to be a mixture of a deep smooth maroon or dark purple hues.

Although this woman was no taller than five foot seven, and Skyler was a solid six feet tall, something about the natural ease and presence with which she carried herself made Skyler feel as though she was actually towering over him even when he had still been standing upright. Skyler was clearly repulsed by the presence of this woman under these circumstances, yet she was so stunning and magnetic that he could not take his eyes off of her. There was something so familiar about her, maybe like someone who had taken care of him when he was young, but for the life of him he just couldn't put his finger on it.

Materializing on the outside of the window to meet Skyler on the street, she inquired softly but firmly, "Well, sweetheart, are you just going to sit there on your ass all day or get it in gear? We have a lot of work to do and a very important dream to discuss." Scurrying back from her again as much as possible with all the thrust he could muster in his fingers and his toes while feeling like he was making as much progress as a cockroach on its back, he yelled, "Who . . . What are you? Did you just walk through that window like it was an open door or am I just really drunk?" Skyler wondered if he was still dreaming. But no, he clearly remembered that he had woken up, paid his tab and left the bar. He knew that he wasn't still dreaming, but he also knew that he was still incredibly drunk. He just hoped that this crazy lady didn't fully kill his buzz before he made it to the bridge.

"You know," the woman mused slowly and deliberately annunciating every syllable like she wanted him to absorb what she was saying, "dreams are a lot like people, matter and energy. They can evolve from a less solid state to a more solid state and back again, but they can never be destroyed. Similarly, you can crush a mirror by dropping a wrecking ball on it, but its images and reflections will live on." Skyler wasn't exactly sure what these statements meant but when she said these words, in his imagination he saw a wrecking ball being dropped from the bridge onto a mirror rather than the water below it and her words vividly reminded him of his own dream that he was trying to outwit at the bridge. So, he spat back, "What are you some kind of fortune teller or something?"

"No, my dear. Mirrors, the puddles and the rivers that you have befriended are more like fortune tellers because they reveal the hatred of yourself that you are projecting into them, and that you are therefore projecting into your future." Then her mannerism shifted slightly to a sly smile, and with a gleam in her eye and a pointer finger raised as if to single herself out, she continued, "But I, my love, am more of a fortune *maker*, as you will soon come to discover!"

Her perceptiveness made Skyler feel exposed and he quickly heard himself mutter in response, "I don't . . . hate myself." But this comment only drew a raised and questioning eyebrow from the lady and even he himself was embarrassed by his lack of certainty and sputtering enthusiasm. "Well, maybe you don't," she humbly conceded before going on, "I suppose no one really hates oneself. Most people have never even met the magnificence of themselves and if they have, they have simply stopped listening to their hearts. But one must never stop listening to their heart," she began this last sentence with so much passion in her voice that it almost reminded Skyler of a singer coming to the climax of a song before she continued on, more humorously now, "because as I like to say, 'the head is bigger but the heart is infinitely more powerful,' and unfortunately, if a person stops listening to their heart, their heart will stop speaking to them," she mused reflectively, almost as if she had forgotten that Skyler was there and was simply speaking to herself.

But then, as if coming to herself again and focusing on the matter at hand, she redirected her attention to the dazed and somewhat petrified man below her as he sat there on the ground with his palms stretched out behind him and his knees still bent as if he wanted to be prepared to scurry further away at a moments notice.

"In your case though, your heart has not stopped speaking to you. The dream keeps coming, does it not?" she asked rhetorically with another sly smile. Knowingly she went on, "But you have merely began interpreting the dream as being antagonistic towards you." This last comment touched a nerve within Skyler, and he fired back with heated energy, "What do you expect? My dream is so unattainable that it's painful. It's so clear and inviting that I leave everything to follow it but as soon as I do, the reality of it becomes so elusive, grand, untouchable and fleeting as a castle of clouds parading in the sky!"

"Well honey, you didn't think that such a fantastic dream as the one that you had would materialize without any character building in the process, did you?" she interrogated with her shoulders shrugged and both eyebrows raised. Seeing his sheepish look, she went on, "Listen, dreams are not so much hard to get as they are seductive and enjoy *playing* hard to get. When you know that the universe is playful, you will take her suggestiveness as proof of interest and simply enjoy the games, the hints and the dreams that she sends you while giving the universe space to let her reveal everything to you at just the right time."

"The universe loves the process of what you become in the chasing of your dreams and uses the time and the experience to align and develop your backbone in full harmony, accordance and alignment with your wishbone, as Claude Bristol likes to say. He says that the power of imagination that is in each of us is as dynamic as TNT that can clear away any mountainous obstacles in its path. However, he reiterates, 'You have got to have a wishbone backed up with a backbone and that isn't all – the wishbone and the backbone must be coordinated and synchronized to a point where they are running in perfect harmony, and when they are in tune, you will find personality developing.'[4] This developing personality will cause you to begin giving yourself what I call, 'A daily dosage of positive energy that's so corrosive that it wears out every negative doubt as the gap between the dream and reality closes.'"

The woman continued with no less intensity, "Again, every wish needs to bud and develop strong wings from its back before it can learn to take flight." To this Skyler cut her off, rolling his eyes in sarcastic protest, "Oh, another wings fanatic, huh?" "Don't be naïve, my dear," The woman responded, "it's a sign of immaturity to treat as literal what was merely meant as a literary device. What would the world be without the power of story and the magic of the myth? What would it be without *The Beauty and The Beast, The Tortoise and The Hare, The Ugly Duckling?* Of course people don't grow wings and turtles don't beat rabbits in real life, but people do undergo radical transformations from hardships to safe havens, sickness to wholeness, from living lost to living leadership, from being bound to breaking free, from dying of depression to dominating in life, from mental shadiness to enlightenment, from difficulties to the fulfillment of desires, from mental captivity to eliminating limitations, from drowning to surfing and from poverty to palaces."

"There's nothing wrong with people using wings and other human enhancing traits to symbolize the magic of metamorphosis, the transition from tragedy into the good life, or to symbolize the ability to do now what was once impossible. Psychologically speaking, spiritual teacher Richard Rohr warns that, 'If we don't learn to mythologize our lives, inevitably we will pathologize them.'[5] This means that if we can't find connections from our stories in the parallel themes of the overarching stories of literary myths, our mental disorders alone will be the repetitive and inescapable theme in the stories of our lives." Skyler thought within himself that he certainly knew what it was to live in mental chaos, but he had read and been transfixed by thousands of books and stories and none of them ever seemed to help him to escape from his despair for more than a few hours. So, he wondered within himself if she could possibly be right and if so, why the power of story never previously had the same therapeutic effects on him.

The woman went on, "Just because you haven't experienced the importance of metamorphosis yet, my dear, does not mean that you are not on the verge of it at this very moment. It takes time to develop but if we let the mystery of this developmental process become a distraction, we may miss the artistic masterpiece of our own self-mastery. As the imaginative creator of *Narnia* once wrote, 'It is not like teaching a horse to jump better and better, but like turning a horse into a winged creature. Of course, once it has got its wings, it will soar over fences, which could never have been jumped and thus beat the natural horse at its own game. But there may be a period, while the wings are just beginning to grow, when it cannot do so: and at that stage the lumps on the shoulders—no one could tell by looking at them that they are going to be wings—may even give it an awkward appearance.'[6] However, no matter how awkward you may feel while developing your wings, which you are doing right now, my love, you have to have a never-say-die attitude! You can take breaks, but if you quit, your developing wings will never see the light of day and the universe and everyone in it will never see the magic that you came here to mesmerize us with. As I like to say, 'You'll always be curious yet deliriously sinking into whatever your nightmare is, until you let your wings know you're serious by leaping into your wildest dreams of self love.'"

"Yeah well, I've tried leaping into my dreams on several occasions and it never works. So, it's time to try something else," Skyler said referring to the leap he was planning for later without wanting to reveal too much.

"I hear what you're saying loud and clear but think about it, my dear! Although impossible dreams do indeed come true, it doesn't even happen quickly in the fairytales, myths and movies," she said, quite matter-of-factly. Redoubling the compassion in her tone she then said, "Sweetheart, life certainly isn't all about the struggle but you've got to admit that Pinocchio, Cinderella and Odysseus would have hardly had stories to tell and wouldn't have given us the delightful inspiration that has stood the test of time without a few hard knocks sprinkled in with the magical fairy dust that each of their stories hold, now would they?" Skyler shrugged apathetically not wanting to admit defeat so easily. Flashing her eyebrows at him in a flirtatious way now, she mused, "Since it takes time for the universe to fully reveal herself to the one who dreams and enduring this patience produces wisdom, I like to say it this way, 'They say a woman is a crockpot meaning she likes to be pursued. Well wisdom is the same, it takes time to unveil her truths.'"

Inexplicably, this woman piqued Skyler's interest and he felt something that he hadn't felt in years while he found himself doing something that he hadn't done in lifetimes. He smiled. At this, the woman also smiled, held out her hand to help him up and invited him in for a warm drink. Even though he admitted inwardly to himself that he did indeed hate himself, he hated his life and hated what he'd become, somehow he knew with certainty that he liked this woman and he figured at this point that he had nothing to lose by spending a little time with this mysterious stranger.

For some reason, Skyler felt that the woman's voice and her words, although gypsyesque and scattered at times, were almost as dazzling as she was, or maybe even more brilliant than she was. Although, when he thought about it, this seemed impossible to Skyler. In the same way that there was no rhyme nor reason to most of the stars that had been peppered here and there throughout space and scattered across the sky, yet these same stars kept their ability to dazzle the simplest of minds throughout every era of time, there was a seductive pull on her words that kept him similarly transfixed though he couldn't always decipher their logic or penetrate their meaning.

Even still, Skyler felt like each of her words was a diamond in the sky that she'd left behind for him to grasp as he swung from rung to rung like a child swinging playfully on playground bars, reaching out towards, clasping tightly and then following her every word on a starry night into a galaxy of this new thought system. He had no idea who this lady was nor how she seemed to know him better than he knew himself. He didn't know how he'd gotten mixed up with her, nor did he have any clue where any of this was leading, but some irresistible force compelled him to accompany her inside.

3 THE COFFEE SHOP

The familiar smooth aromas of different blends of quality coffee gripped Skyler and enticed him to a cup upon entering the spacious shop. However, when the woman offered him a large black mug of it from behind the bar, he responded by saying, "I was hoping for something a little warmer going down, if you know what I mean?" Raising an eyebrow, the woman said, "I thought you might!" And with that, she reached down and disappeared below the counter before reemerging with a bottle of dark rum in one hand and a bottle of Kahlua coffee liqueur in the other. Smiling from ear to ear, Skyler said, "Now you're speaking my language!" as the woman poured and mixed one Café Don Juan topped with grated chocolate for Skyler and one topped with whipped cream and grated chocolate for herself.

As she made the drinks, Skyler noticed that the place was filled with two things that aren't in every coffee shop: plants and books. On each side of the bar there were bookshelves from floor to ceiling extending to the front of the store on his left and to the back of the shop on his right. However, it was difficult to get a good look at most of the titles from where he sat not only because of the distance separating him from the books but also because Devil's Ivy covered and wove around the top of the bookshelves. It had also begun invading, crawling and interweaving its leaves amongst the many tiers of it. There were large plants on the floors in the corners of the shop and smaller ones with colorful and exotic flowers on various tables throughout, though not every table bore the beautiful foliage.

However, Skyler was more interested in the books than the plants because of his passion for literature. When he was young, he actually wanted to be a teacher so that he could share his love for story and his love of learning with the budding minds of tomorrow. That kind of job would not be work to him. But as he grew older, he left his dreams of teaching as he moved in pursuit of jobs that were more financially stable for his ever-expanding family. He also noticed that the coffee shop was spacious, and it only looked more so because of the mirror that covered the whole wall that was behind him as he sat at the coffee bar. There were more couches and knee high coffee tables than there were chairs with regular standing tables. The lights were dim, and the mood was Zen as he usually found it to be in most of the cafés that he had visited.

As they came away from the bar opting to sit with their coffee at one of the tables with chairs rather than in one of the couch areas, the woman asked, "Where were we?" referring to their conversation that they were having outside the storefront. Skyler said, "I think you were talking about waiting for dreams to come true because they can often take more time than expected." "Yes, my dear, I remember now, that's exactly where we were," she said while gathering her thoughts. "I am going to shift our discussion slightly right now because I want to share a little more about the process of creating rather than continuing on about the process of waiting." Skyler nodded, shrugged slightly and said, "Ok."

She went on, "In speaking of those who are prone to getting stuck in poor cycles of thinking, Friedrich Nietzsche once said, and I'm paraphrasing here, 'Sometimes it's easy for a person to feel like a tree in that the more one's limbs stretch to the sky, the deeper their roots are thrust down into the earth.'[7] This image portrays one who is excited by achievement and simultaneously rooted to the familiar and the mundane. But on the flip side of being stagnant and frustrated, Nietzsche's ideas also indicated that 'It was the height of a person's journey through life to move through a threefold metamorphosis of positive transformation. The journey begins as a camel that slaves away under systems that it did not create. Then turning into a lion, it begins to destroy those burdensome systems. And finally, it morphs into a freethinking and innocent human child who lives and creates its own values. This child is likened to a wheel that spins and spawns its own magical momentum in the sport of creating its own world.'[8] This is a process that I call, 'the quest to create.'"

Then inquiring of Skyler once again she asked, "Do you, at this moment in your life, my dear shadow boxer," referring to Skyler's scuffle with his shadow outside on the street, "feel more like the growing tree which is simultaneously fated with its roots throwing themselves down into the depths of the earth? Or are you the lively child who is rolling and racing freely across a tightrope from success to success and mountaintop to mountaintop?" Skyler was familiar with Nietzsche's fables that the woman quoted and thought that they were interesting, but he honestly had no idea what they had to do with his reoccurring dream.

Skyler knew that he looked as disheveled as he felt after his encounter with the bus and the bar. In addition to this, he was still feeling the burn on his palms and fingers from scurrying back from the woman on the pavement outside. His mind was also flashing back to falling from the curb into the puddle and flashing forward to falling from the bridge towards the river. So, the Skyler wrung his hands soothing the discomfort from them and stubbornly asked, "Which image do you think I feel closer to? You seem to always know what I'm thinking about anyway. Meanwhile, I don't even know your name!" Skyler genuinely felt cornered and like the woman's question was unfair considering the circumstances.

True to form, the woman responded in a round about way saying, "Well, sugar, we have a saying where I come from that says, 'The harder a baby cries, the sweeter it dreams.'"

"What's that supposed to mean?" Skyler wondered out loud as he was taken aback by the obvious obscurity of her words.

"I'm saying that if we learn to cross them properly, the rivers that we cry can lead us to oceans of invincible happiness. As the mystical poet Rumi likes to say, 'where there is ruin, there is hope for a treasure,'[9] and as I like to say, 'you see yourself as a shipwreck, but we see your treasure glowing inside, beneath the oceans in your eyes.' But returning to Nietzsche's images, as long as you see yourself as a tree or anything else that is symbolic to you of being stuck in a downward cycle, the heights that you climb will be forever subject to the perpetual cycles of gravity and the downward motions that you are fixed upon. However, as you begin to see yourself as a child of invincible happiness, limitless treasures and creative genius, you will sail from success to success in a ship that was engineered by the new blueprints that you yourself have designed."

The woman's words were so tantalizing and imaginative to Skyler that even though they both remained firmly planted in the coffee shop, her language would often elevate his consciousness and take him to some strange scene where he would actually observe a cinematic unfolding of her words in action. For instance, when she said, "The harder a baby cries, the sweeter it dreams," Skyler's mind became aware of a picturesque hologram of a baby crying in a crib within the baby's room. Then the scene seamlessly shifted so that Skyler could see the content of the baby's dreams of floating balloons attached to that baby's wrist, which were gently carrying it off into the clouds. All of this causing the sleeping baby a wide-eyed excitement at his new explorations in his dreams, which simultaneously caused the baby sporadic smiles in its crib while it slept.

When the woman said, "You see yourself as a shipwreck but we see your treasure glowing inside, beneath the oceans in your eyes," Skyler was transported to the site of a fierce storm on the seas where he was thrown into the drama of a capsizing ship that was sinking to the bottom of the ocean. After the ship crashed into the ocean floor and settled into the sand, Skyler found himself with the woman snorkeling through its many passage ways before opening a secret vault filled with tons of diamonds, rubies, silver and gold. Sometimes these images would simply flash into his mind in a rapid burst of understanding that he was able to capture while she was still speaking her sentence at a normal pace.

At other times, these visions would lead to greater questions and it seemed that everything would slow down so drastically that Skyler would forget that she was even speaking as he would be carried away with her on the river of her imagery, taking in the full scope of that one vision and exploring its psychological landscape for what felt like hours on end. The images were so vivid and felt so real that Skyler wondered if the gypsy woman had slipped something into his drink. But he was so swept up into the scenery of these stories, and he felt so good that the thought just seemed to be a petty distraction that was too far below him to capture his attention for any meaningful amount of time.

"By the way, darling," the woman said, "my name . . . my name is Zenith." Temporarily coming back down somewhat, Skyler nodded thankfully and said in an incomplete manner as if not fully satisfied, "Ok, Zenith." Normally this would be the time in a conversation that Skyler would return the favor with his own name. However, he had an annoying suspicion that Zenith already knew his name and of course, as expected, she didn't ask for it.

Zenith went on, "This transformation that I speak of, or becoming a child of infinite happiness, comes from fixing empowering images in your mind, giving yourself new dreams and letting the universe permeate through you to brew these images into the cup of your life. There is an intriguing video featuring Denzel Washington, Lady Gaga, Jim Carey, the boxer Conor McGregor and others about how these famous actors, athletes and musical geniuses followed their dreams and rose to stardom. In one of the scenes, actor and former hip-hop artist Will Smith says, 'Just decide what it's going be, who you're going be, how you're going to do it. Just decide and then from that point, the universe is going to get out of your way. It's water, it wants to move and go around stuff.'[10] He's exactly right in speaking of the rigid obstacles that can and will magically melt and move from your path in your quest to create."

"But there is another way in which the universe is like water. As mentioned previously, our thoughts, imaginations and expectations that we choose are like selecting the type and boldness of coffee grounds that we want to brew. The universe is like water because no matter who we conceive ourselves to be, it flows through our internal concepts of ourselves and steams the visions and images of our dreams that we hold in our minds right into the cup of our lives, which we consume as the external reality that we've internally set to be brewed into being."

"Motivational speaker Zig Ziglar once said, 'Somebody asked Helen Keller (a phenomenal woman who was both deaf and blind) what would be worse than being blind. Without hesitation, she said, 'It would be infinitely worse to have perfect eyesight and no vision than the other way around.'[11] Her vision of who she wanted to be was crystal clear in her mind even though she was blind. Through that vision, she was able to give greater vision to millions of people. This is true because it's the vision that we hold on the inside that propels our direction in our outside world."

"She could have focused on all of the ways that life screwed her over, but she realized as I love to say that, 'Some situations are just like bad dreams. They're only unbearable while we're giving them our full attention.' She realized that she could not annihilate her fate by constantly thinking of all the ways in which she thought that she had been fated because the boldness of those grounds would have become the flavor that the universe filtered into the cup of her life. If the taste of your life is bitter, you must simply select a new blend of fresh images for the universe to filter through you."

"In this way, you will not focus on the puddles that life presents you with, because indeed, 'Life *is* a gloomy puddle, until you start jumping in it.'" When Zenith said this last saying, the table between her and Skyler stretched itself into an executive fountain park that local employees on lunch break began dancing and frolicking around in without a care in the world like some unexpected flash mob. Completely surprised by the people in the vision making utter fools of themselves, all in the name of having a good time, Skyler smirked as he also thought of Helen Keller's story of triumph.

Momentarily distracted by this vision, Skyler was oblivious to his earlier encounter with the crowd, the swerving bus and his hatred of his own reflection in the puddle. However, seeing his smile as an indication that he was genuinely seeing and tracking her words, Zenith continued, "Rather you will focus on the invincible happiness of the destiny that you seek to attain. As Socrates in *Way Of The Peaceful Warrior* says, 'The secret of change is to focus all of your energy, not on fighting the old but on building the new.'"[12]

"That makes sense." Skyler replied nonchalantly before taking a swig of coffee.

4 THE DREAM

Taking a sip from her cup, looking up intently at Skyler with one eyebrow raised, she said, "Your dream was so simple and so clear. Yet, as you will soon see, it was packed with grounds, images and concepts for your filter." "Yeah," Skyler replied, "I still don't know how you could know what I have been dreaming about and I was wondering when you were even going to tie everything that you have been talking about together with my dream. However, I figured that you would get there eventually though, and I am all ears if you're ready to go there now."

"Yes darling!" Zenith explained, "I wanted to first set the tone with some preliminary discussion on the importance of using your vision to create your life. But now that I have whet your appetite a little, I would like to discuss this phenomenal dream that has been given to you!" She paused for a moment sipping her cup and Skyler used the opportunity to inquire, "Well, where should we begin?"

To his astonishment, Zenith answered his question by directly explaining the contents of his dream, "Except for the very first time that you had this dream, which prompted you to dream bigger and move on from that first position many years ago, every time that you had the dream, was just after you quit your day job. Each time, you were standing in the common area of your office where you worked in the dream but had just resigned from in real life. A woman who you didn't actually know or even recognize but gave you the sense and impression of representing someone who worked with you in the dream, was also in the office standing with you."

"Suddenly a mysterious man walked in and said, 'There is a man outside who has something for both of you!' Together, you and the woman tell him to tell the man who is standing outside that he can come on in. The man comes in and tells you that someone has died and has left two envelopes for you. The stranger then says that one envelope was for the lady standing next to you and the other one was for you, before promptly delivering each envelope to you and your supposed co-worker."

"The man and his associate then leave with no explanation of who died nor why this person has left you each an envelope. Turning to you, the lady says, 'Let's take a walk down the hall.' You head out together and getting to a quiet location that you used to go to in order to make phone calls in real life, she says to you, 'The man who died was loaded, so I know that I'm going to be set for life.' You were excited for her but still having no idea what to expect for yourself since you had no clue who the man that died was, you replied by saying, 'Why don't you go ahead and open it?' She opens it and finds a check made out to her for $40 million. The world shifts before you and the ground shifts beneath you as you realized the gravity of what has just happened for her, you begin to wonder what the future holds for you and what any of this could possibly mean. Then she looks to you and says, 'See, I told you!' and gestures to your envelope suggesting that you open it."

"You open it and there within it is a twin check made out to you for $40 million! That part gives me chills just thinking about it," Zenith said before going on "but the feeling that you got from the dream was threefold. You had two distinct feelings in the dream and one overwhelming feeling after waking. The first feeling that you had in the dream was astonishment that someone had finally recognized your work and your passion for what you do to help people and you felt that that person had decided to reward you generously."

"The second feeling that you had in the dream was honestly one of overwhelming fear and terror that you had this amount of money in your possession. Even though it was a check with your name on it, not cash, you literally feared for your life with an impending doom that your life was in serious danger. Even though you'd never met one, you felt that this is what a jackpot lottery winner must feel before one is safely able to turn in their winning ticket. Then you awoke from the dream in the midst of trying to safely sneak out of work in order to get your newfound fortune to a bank where it would be more secure."

Baffled by this retelling of his most intimate thoughts and most protected secret, Skyler shouted in utter amazement, "Who are you and how could you possibly know all of that! This is crazy!" "Well darling, you could just say that it's a gift that I've been developing for some time," Zenith said. "But just wait, my friend!" she continued, "You may be infinitely more shocked at the interpretation of the dream because, if you can grasp it, as Eckhart Tolle suggests, you will become an alchemist that can transmute and mine extraordinary treasures from the base metal of what now seems to be a basic and ordinary life."[13]

Zenith paused briefly before continuing, in order to take a sip of her coffee and to let her words sink in. "Now, do you remember the feeling that you had after you awoke that first time that you had this dream?" "Of course, I do!" Skyler shot back excitedly. Then looking down initially and rubbing the back of his neck, he added, "Even though, I guess I've seriously grown jaded by that unattainable feeling that I spoke of earlier, initially the dream was pure magic and the feeling that it gave me was genuinely one that I will never forget!"

Reenergized and enthused by Zenith's unfathomable capabilities, Skyler went on, "Once I was back in reality and was no longer afraid of my gift being taken . . . I guess I never really had it in the first place," Skyler thought aloud before continuing on. "The feeling I got from the dream was that for the first time in my life I had gotten paid the type of money that I was worth!" Skyler's face flushed with embarrassment as he said these bizarre words. Then attempting to justify himself he said, "When I said that I'd gotten paid what I was worth, I didn't mean in relation to the work that I'd been doing at my job . . . It's kind of hard to explain, but . . ."

"Go on. I'm listening," Zenith reassured.

Skyler resumed, "It really had nothing to do with work at all. It had more to do with my overall value, worth and significance as a person. I know that it might sound a little crazy, maybe over the top or even grandiose but I once heard a motivational speaker at a business conference that I had to attend for work who was talking about the outrageous costs of medical operations that different people had to undergo in order to replace vital organs, limbs, vital fluids, female eggs and other body parts. The totals added up to ridiculous and outrageous sums. I guess before then, I had never given much thought to the value of our physical body parts."

Skyler continued, "Even though, to say that I don't always demonstrate it, would be an understatement, that discussion on the actual price of our physical value alone convinced me that each of us is far more valuable than I had ever expected. Not to mention parts of our bodies like the brain which we haven't even discovered how to transplant yet and our non-physical value such as the love, the good times shared between companions and the unique ideas and thoughts that each of us holds within us." Zenith sat there and stared at Skyler, marveling at how all of his previous apathy seemed to have evaporated. She also sat there appreciating how he had obviously stumbled upon a topic that caused him to light up.

Skyler could tell that Zenith was reflecting on the recent shift in his mood as he continued, "Anyway, that feeling of receiving the check was absolutely exhilarating and at first my mind oscillated back and forth between whether the universe was telling me that this dream would actually take place in reality or whether it would not actually take place but was simply a mere dream given to me so that I could experience what it felt like to be valued and appreciated at the highest level. Lately though, I have been wondering if this dream is just the universe's way of playing a cruel joke on me," Skyler said, concluding his trail of thought in genuine confusion.

5 AN ORACLE OF GOOD THINGS TO COME

"I can see how you have come to feel this way, my dear," Zenith responded before going on. "But you will come to discover everything you seek in perfect timing, my love. However, addressing this uncertainty concerning your two initial interpretations is a great place for us to begin before we actually get to the deeper meaning of the dream itself. Let me speak concerning this internal debate that you mentioned, but before I do, I want you to remember that feeling of finally getting paid what you are worth because you must make that feeling a part of the fresh new blend that you place in your filter."

"From now on, only pour these feelings that emotionally thrill and mentally stimulate you into your filter, and I promise that the taste of life that you produce will be rich and smooth." Mulling it over, Skyler contentedly took in the fabulous feelings that he had initially encountered in the dream once again as Zenith proceeded. "Now, back to your internal debate between this dream being a foretelling of good things to come or whether it was simply a dream concerning your self worth. I have found, when presented with two incredible options, that the complexity of life usually allows for a middle way answer of both-and, rather than one that forces us to choose an answer of either-or."

"Through personal experience, I have also come to realize that we will experience in reality whatever we persist in setting our minds upon, regardless of whether we set our minds upon what is desirable or something unfavorable. What I mean is this. If you were to simply believe that what happened to you in this dream would never happen in real life, you would be setting the wheels in motion for it to never happen because the mind is extremely magnetic."

"In what way is the mind magnetic?" Skyler asked.

"Oh, there are millions of real life stories that prove that the mind is magnetic including one of your own. But for now, I'll share these three short stories about how people have magnetized their minds to attract their dream jobs, which should make it overwhelmingly clear."

Skyler's curiosity was catapulted into a sky of a thousand questions at Zenith's suggestion that one of his own stories could prove that the mind had magnetic powers but he could see in her eyes that Zenith was eager to move on and he knew that her thought process was like a meandering river that would eventually lead to the sea, maybe a waterfall or some other spectacular sight if he'd only let it. So, he trusted the process and temporarily bit his tongue on this subject, holding his questions for now as Zenith began. "First, there was a comic strip writer named Scott Adams who got his start back in the early 1990s. Henriette Anne Klauser shares Adams' story in a book that she wrote in 2001 called *Write It Down, Make It Happen: Knowing What You Want & Getting It*. Now, the title of her book alone is a master key to success that could eradicate unhappiness from the earth if people took it seriously or even played around with it more. But I'm getting off topic. In her book, Klauser tells Adams' tale saying,

> As a lowly technology worker in a cubicle in corporate America, Adams kept doodling at his office desk. Then, he began to write, fifteen times a day, "I will become a syndicated cartoonist." Through many rejections he persevered and finally it happened: he signed a contract for his strip to be syndicated. That's when he started writing, "I will be the best cartoonist on the planet." How to judge that? Well Dilbert is syndicated in almost 2,000 newspapers worldwide. The Dilbert Zone website gets 100,000 visitors a day. Adam's first book, The Dilbert Principle, sold more than 1.3 million copies. Products from mouse pads to coffee cups to desk calendars based on the Dilbert characters are everywhere, and there is even a weekly TV show. Now Scott Adams writes fifteen times a day, "I will win a Pulitzer Prize."[14]

"That's pretty amazing," Skyler said pensively.

"Indeed, it is," Zenith agreed. "His story is compelling evidence that you do in fact magnetically bring about what you think about, as the old saying goes."

"Next there is the story of Jack Canfield, the *Chicken Soup for The Soul* author, as he shares his story in the well-known book by Rhonda Byrne called *The Secret*. Canfield says that he was making $8,000 a year when he met his mentor named W. Clement Stone. Stone told him that he could become whatever he wants by simply visualizing his goal as if it was already achieved. Jack put his mentor to the test by setting his intention to make $100,000 that year. Soon after, Jack created a $100,000 check made out to himself that he placed on his ceiling so that he would see it every morning upon waking. That year he got an idea to sell 400,000 copies of his books at twenty-five cents each although he still had no idea how to do that."

"One day while in the grocery line he noticed a magazine ad and he got another idea that if he could simply get the right ad in a magazine, he could sell 400,000 copies of his book. Later on, that year, while speaking at an event, a writer from that exact same magazine that he had seen earlier heard him speak and she asked if she could interview him. Canfield says, that year he attracted speaking gigs and book sales that skyrocketed his earnings from $8,000 a year to $92,327. Further, he used the same technique to help craft the mega-selling book series *Chicken Soup for The Soul* that brought him everything that he had been dreaming of with his newly set intentions.[15]

"That's . . . really interesting," Skyler said, visibly stirred by the story.

"Exactly!" Zenith continued, "These stories not only signify the magnetic nature of our thoughts, but they also affirm, as Bob Proctor concludes that, 'If you can hold it in your head, you can hold it in your hand.'"[16] "Finally," Zenith went on, "all of this is no different than what Jim Carey did when he wrote himself a check for $10 million."

"Oh yeah," Skyler cut in. "I heard about how he wrote that check to himself long before he ever had any serious acting gigs. Are you talking about how he put it in his pocket for a few years and kept working towards his dream before he actually got the news that he would be receiving a real check for that exact amount on one of his early movies?"[17]

Zenith nodded before Skyler went on, "That story is magical, but I guess it makes even more sense to me now that I'm finding that others are using similar techniques to do similar things."

Zenith nodded and repeated the title of Klauser's book pointedly as if it was so simple that this short phrase could cure all of Skyler's problems and end world hunger in a single breath. "*Write It Down and Make It Happen:* Know What You Want and Get It,'" Zenith said, "You see, it's the miracle minded who become the miracle magnets, and those who refuse to take no for an answer are often the ones who receive the most magically unexpected yesses."

Zenith continued, "So again, my dear, your mind is so magnetic that if you were to simply believe that what happened to you in this dream would never happen in real life, you would be setting the wheels in motion for the dream to never take place because wherever your presence is, there your future will be also. On the other hand, if you just as easily believed in and set your mind, your emotions and your will on the reality of this event actually occurring in your life as countless others have done concerning their own visions of success, you would be setting the wheels in motion to roll the dice of these unusual and prosperous circumstances into the internal and external life of your present and future conditions. In other words, by believing positively or negatively, we are setting the wheels of time in motion for the events in our mind to roll right into our future lives."

Skyler pondered deeply for a bit and then he said, "There is obviously a pattern and a power in these stories that is undeniable. But they just seem so mysterious that I'm not really sure that I understand it or can put my finger on the mechanics of what has happened in each of these stories. I mean, I could easily retell these stories to someone else but if they asked me how it all works, I'd be at a loss for words," Skyler admitted. Zenith looked at Skyler with understanding and said slowly as if gathering her thoughts to approach the issue from a previously unexplored angle, "Ok. Let me see if I can clear things up a bit with a quote by the New Thought philosopher Wallace D. Wattles. Then we'll see if we can connect what he is saying about nature of the universe with what, Scott Adams, Jack Canfield and Jim Carrey have all demonstrated in their lives."

Skyler snickered briefly at the name Wallace Wattles, unable to suppress a bit of laughter before responding, "Works for me. But before we go there, I have to ask, "What is New Thought?" Smiling back at Skyler and validating his childish humor before proceeding, Zenith said, "New Thought is a philosophy that asserts that every invention and every situation and even the world itself is made through conscious or unconscious thought, attention and intentions. Therefore, it posits that anyone can have a new life if they can shift their consciousness to a firmly fixed new thought that drives out old and tired ways of thinking. Does that make sense?"

"Had I not heard those previous stories, I'd be lost right now, but seems simple enough in light of everything that we've already talked about," Skyler shrugged.

"Perfect!" Zenith said before moving on to the promised quote and playfully reiterating the philosopher's funny name, which only provoked more laughter from Skyler. "Wallace D. Wattles says, 'There is a thinking stuff from which all things are made and which in its original state permeates, penetrates and fills the inner spaces of the universe. A thought in this substance produces the thing that is imaged by the thought. A person can form things in one's thought and by impressing this thought upon formless substance can cause the thing one thinks about to be created . . . you must dwell upon this until it is fixed in your mind and has become your habitual thought.'[18]

"That's an intriguing concept," Skyler said as his mind worked to puzzle it all together with the previous stories. Zenith went on, "Notice that all of the people in the stories that I have just offered you were completely focused on the destination that they both dreamed about and were determined to arrive at to the exclusion of all else. They weren't thinking about 'if' they could accomplish their dreams but 'when' they would accomplish their dreams. They weren't thinking about 'how' they could accomplish it but only how they could keep the vision of what they wanted firmly fixed in each of their minds through writing it, affirming it and visualizing it. In this way, they were all radiating a new reality and living in the reality that they had imagined with complete disregard for what others might have said was impossible. This is what I call living in the consciousness of accomplishment because it reorients our mind to our own personal vision of success and trains us to remain there until an exact replica of our goal is established in our world."

"The reason that each of the people in the previous examples could be so certain of their intended outcomes was because they knew the secret of the universe. That secret says exactly what Wallace Wattles was saying, which is that the whole universe is made of thought substance and you can influence the creation of a new world with the creation of a new and focused thought. When you do this, you are focusing on the feeling of your wish fulfilled and the universe must respond to you in kind by giving physical form to the formless imagination that you have pressed upon it. Stamp the universe with your imagination and the universe will stamp you with the badge of success. Use your imagination to impact the invisible realm of infinite possibilities and the infinite realm of possibilities will impact you with a new reality. All you need is a pinch of imagination in order to awaken to the reality of your dreams. Consider the words of the mystical genius Neville Goddard who dedicated his life to helping others to live into their highest ideals of themselves. He says:

> *You, assuming the feeling of your wish fulfilled and continuing therein, take upon yourself the results of that state. Not assuming the feeling of your wish fulfilled, you are ever free of the results . . . When you can call up at will whatsoever image you please, when the forms of your imagination are as vivid to you as the forms of nature, you are master of your fate . . . The law of assumption is the means by which the fulfillment of your desires may be realized. Every moment of your life, consciously or unconsciously, you are assuming a feeling. You can no more avoid assuming a feeling than you can avoid eating and drinking. All you can do is control the nature of your assumptions. Thus, it is clearly seen that the control of your assumption is the key you now hold to an ever-expanding, happier, more noble life.*[19]

Skyler mused, "We usually use the word 'assume' with negative connotations. But it seems that this Neville character is using the words 'assume' and 'assumptions' in a positive way. It seems that he is using these words almost as if one should assume a feeling just as one dons a coat."

"Yes!" Zenith replied emphatically before continuing on, "And taking it a step further, I would say that just as easy as a person puts on a raincoat and opens their umbrella before stepping out on a rainy day, you too must put on a new concept of yourself and never take it off, nor pull the umbrella of your imagination down until you see the sun shining on the new situation that you have imagined. You must never be convinced that you are being drenched in your old reality, regardless of how much others are absorbed in it. What is true for them is not true for you, because they are not living in your world. They are not living in your raincoat nor are they living beneath the umbrella of consciousness that you have raised. They may be completely soaked in their world while you remain poised and untouched by unfavorable conditions in your own."

"Further, the dream that you were given has actually put you one step ahead of the game in regard to 'assuming the feeling of your wish fulfilled' as Neville Goddard says, because you already know exactly what it felt like to have what you desire. You felt electrified with the feelings of your own self worth. You felt that you had finally gotten paid what you were worth. And you felt as though you had just won the lottery. Because you have seen it with your own eyes, you now know that somewhere in the universe there is a check for $40 million with your name on it. In regard to your dream, you must, as the mystic philosopher says, 'Assume the feeling of your wish fulfilled' and keep that positive memory firmly fixed in your mind. As I always say, 'In order to live fully, you must be guided by the reality of your ecstasy more than the maintenance of your monotony.'"

"If you can bear it, take one last example in the life of Lou Holtz as described again by Henriette Anne Klauser in the same book that I mentioned earlier."

Skyler chimed in and asked, *"Write It Down, Make It Happen?"*

"Exactly, my dear!" Zenith replied with a smile before continuing. "In it, she says,

Lou Holtz, the famous football coach, did this in 1966. He was twenty-eight years old when he sat down at his dining

room table and wrote out one hundred and seven impossible goals. He had just lost his job, he had no money in the bank, and his wife, Beth, was 8 months pregnant with their third child. He was so discouraged that Beth gave him a copy of The Magic of Thinking Big by David J. Schwartz to help lift his spirits. Up until then, Holtz says, he was totally lacking in motivation.

"There are so many people, and I was one of them, who don't do anything special with their lives. The book said you should write down all the goals you wanted to achieve before you died."

The goals he wrote in answer to that challenge were both personal and professional. Most seemed impossible to a twenty-eight-year-old out-of-work man. His list included having dinner at the White House, appearing on the Tonight Show, meeting the pope, becoming head coach at Notre Dame, winning a national championship, being coach of the year, landing on an aircraft carrier, making a hole in one and jumping out of an airplane.

If you check out coach Lou Holtz's website, along with this list you will get pictures—pictures of Holtz with the pope, with President Ronald Regan at the White House, yukking it up with Johnny Carson. In addition, a description of what it was like to jump out of an airplane and get not one but two holes in one. Of the one hundred and seven goals on his list from 1966, Lou Holtz has achieved eighty-one. So, give yourself permission to dream, to be totally unrealistic.[20]

"Phenomenal!" Skyler said before concluding, "Coach Lou Holtz is a legendary figure in football, but I never knew his back story or even realized that he came from a place of such struggle.

I've often thought about the source of my own depression in relation to what I guess I'd call a disconnect between knowing that I am capable of so much more yet actually doing so much less. Like Lou Holtz . . ." Skyler fumbled through his thoughts attempting to make a connection. "I guess I've just always desired to do something special with my life, even though I've just always had no clue as to how to make it happen."

Noticing Skyler's piqued interest, Zenith temporarily redirected her focus from the discussion saying, "Oh yeah, inability to find and live out your purpose can be a great source of inner frustration and Lou's experience is really just the tip of the iceberg. There are many people like Lou Holtz who have intriguing stories of going from profound psychological struggle to overwhelming success by simply finding their purpose. Take for instance, Mel Robbins who was so depressed from the loss of her husband's restaurant business and increasing family debt that she couldn't even get herself out of bed day after day. Now however, she's a motivational speaker who's developed and uses her own scientifically and psychologically backed formula that's helped her escape her own paralyzing indecision while helping millions of others make life-affirming decisions of their own so that they can also act on these decisions immediately."[21]

"Eckhart Tolle was so depressed that he couldn't live with himself anymore. When he realized this, he began to ask himself a life-changing question. If *he* couldn't live with *himself* anymore, was there just one of him or actually two? So, stunned by this line of internal questioning, he awakened to his deeper self, which healed his supposed psychological split. Now he guides millions of people in the art of practicing their presence so that they too can disentangle with the depressing thoughts of their life situation and become aware of the delightfulness of their actual life."[22]

"Buckminster Fuller was about to commit suicide in Lake Michigan spurred on by his three-year-old daughter's untimely death and the loss of his company. These two events left him and his family penniless. While contemplating his death at the lake, he heard a voice say, 'From now on you need never await temporal attestation to your thought. You think the truth. You do not have the right to eliminate yourself. You do not belong to you. You belong to the universe. Your significance will remain forever obscure to you, but you may assume that you are fulfilling your role if you apply yourself to converting your experiences to the highest advantage of others.' This experience affected him so much that he set out on a personal experiment to see how much one person with limited resources could make a positive change in his world. Fuller went on to become an author of more than thirty books and became one the great architectural inventors of the 20th Century."[23]

"And finally, when she was seventeen, Marsha Linehan was committed to a psychiatric institution for over two years. A luminous article in The New York Times says that, 'She had tried to kill herself so many times because the gulf between the person she wanted to be and the person she was left her desperate, hopeless, deeply homesick for a life she would never know. That gulf was real and unbridgeable.'[24] While living in what was supposed to be a safe and isolated room where she could no longer cut and burn herself, she began banging her head very hard on both the wall and the floor. Although experts held out no hope of recovery, when Marsha was released from treatment, she had a spiritual experience that completely revolutionized her life."

"Over the past forty-five years Marsha has developed her own uniquely effective and instructional branch of psychology. In it, she uses mindfulness and meditation practices mixed with behavioral psychology to help self-harming and suicidal patients with the most severe personality disorders. Through her therapy, her clients come to cultivate healing and life-change through radical acceptance of themselves. Further, psychologists and students of psychology study and implement Marsha's transformative processes to bring similar benefits to their clients all around the world."

"The list goes on, my love. But Byron Katie, Jim Kwik and Amy Cuddy are also just a few more noteworthy and inspiring examples of people who have endured various forms of psychological brokenness and ruin, but who have nevertheless all transcended their debilitating limitations and have gone on to do amazing things which have impacted millions of people for the better. These ordinary people with extraordinary stories are all demonstrations of the truth that novelist Fyodor Dostoyevsky voiced over a century ago when he said, 'The mystery of human existence lies not in just staying alive, but in finding something to live for.'[25] No matter how big or small the motive, when we find our own unique reason to live, life takes on a new zest that makes the boundaries of our previous life obsolete."

Retracing her steps in order to come back to her previous focus, Zenith said, "I've gotten a bit sidetracked on what I believe is an important tangent from Lou Holtz's story because I wanted to point out how his ability to escape depression was not some lucky anomaly and that even depression itself is no match against the life of one who discovers their own personal meaning and basis for living." Skyler replied, "No . . . I'm actually glad that you did this because although these stories are pretty raw, there's so much within them that I can personally identify with. To get back to your point from earlier, although these stories are far from fairytales, and none of these people have grown wings, they are some real life examples of people who went from devastating circumstances to getting as close to soaring in life as is humanly possible." Zenith replied, "Yes, my dear! Although mind-boggling, none of these stories are unrealistic and neither is hoping for similar experiences in one's own life. They are not only genuine and human, but they are profoundly compelling."

"What I find even more interesting is that Marsha Linehan never even knew how she was going to heal herself nor how she was going to heal others. All she knew was that as she says in her own words, 'I was in hell . . . And I made a vow: when I get out, I'm going to come back and get others out of here.'"[26]

"I want the same thing!" Skyler cried out, "Deep down I've always wanted to help people solve problems that are similar to my own. The only problem is and has always been that as it stands, I can't even help myself." Zenith replied with compassion in her voice, "All it takes is one person to escape from Plato's Cave, in order to bring a host of others out of a world of shadows into a new universe of substance and sunlight."

Zenith continued, "When Linehan was in your shoes, she had no idea how she was going to accomplish her desire. All she knew was that she had the desire. However, the phenomenal news is that holding to the desire of the person of who you want to be assembles the components of that new and ideal personality while you go on about the normal business of your daily life. As I like to say, 'The divine mystery of the mind is that it can manifest mayhem or magic by design as simple as if merely persisting in thinking anything you can imagine makes the law of magnetism active in time.'"

"So, what you're saying is," Skyler concluded, "I simply need to focus on the solutions of the person that I want to be rather than concerning myself with the problems of my current inability to accomplish these desires because I am projecting whatever I'm focusing on?"

"That is exactly what I am saying, my love, as I like to say, 'When you awake in the morning and open your eyes, your level of gratefulness for all that you see will determine whether you perceive problems or whether you perceive a paradise.' And again, 'What we perceive always determines the reality that we will perpetuate.'"

Zenith continued, "It is enough to know that you want to help yourself and help others out of depression. This is a great self-revelation that will serve to give you guidance and direction towards accomplishing your purpose. What you must do is gravitate towards every possible person, book, or thing related to this topic while dropping the rest of your ideas about your inability. Then simply let this concept of your desire form itself around you in time. Your vision will become clearer and clearer as you align with further knowledge and experiences that match your new sense of self. As Zig Ziglar says, 'Go as far as you can see. When you get there, you'll be able to see farther.'[27] And he goes on to say, 'You can have whatever you want in life if you can just help enough other people get what they want.'[28] Focus on your purpose of helping others while visualizing your success and there's no limit to what you can accomplish."

Zenith resumed again where she had broken off, "What I was going to propose earlier about Lou Holtz before I went out on that loose thread of similar stories, was that his magical story of becoming coach of Notre Dame speaks to the reality of just how close we are to the things that we dare to imagine. As philosopher Marcus Aurelius says, 'Do not think that what is hard for you to master is humanly impossible; and if it is humanly possible, consider it to be within your reach.'[29] Shel Silverstein echoes the philosopher's words when he says, 'Listen to the mustn'ts, child. Listen to the don'ts. Listen to the shouldn'ts, the impossibles, the won'ts. Listen to the never haves, then listen close to me. Anything can happen, child. Anything can be.'[30] With your head, heart, guts and every fiber of your being you must come to accept the reality that you can and should block out every voice that doesn't believe in the possibility of your dreams. As I like to say, 'Your fate is never determined when your massive imagination *is*.' Imagination plus determination is the master key that opens the door to new worlds. This, my sweet friend, is how many successful people train themselves to think."

"In fact, Napoleon Hill, the author of *Think & Grow Rich*, the classic guide to drawing wealth, which has been responsible for creating more millionaires than any other book that I have heard of, says that Andrew Carnegie, who was the wealthiest man in America at that time, once told Hill that every person is given two envelopes at birth. Carnegie then went on explaining that all must decide whether they will enjoy the lack, poverty and ill will of the first envelope, or whether they will experience the abundance, good fortune and prosperity of the second.[31] So, according to Carnegie and Hill concerning your dream, you could either rise to your expectations or descend to your doubts, but in the end you would only have yourself and your own mindset to thank for the outcome. Hill goes on to say that, when it comes to living your dream, 'There are no limitations except for the ones that you set up in your own mind or that you permit others to set up for you.'[32] Just as the old adage often attributed to Henry Ford says, 'Whether you think you can or think you can't, you are absolutely right.'[33] Hill goes on to tell the story of this encounter with Carnegie in a well-known video interview called *The Laws of Success*. In it, he says:

'Let me call your attention to a great power, which is under your control.' said Mr. Carnegie. 'A power, which is greater than poverty, greater than the lack of education, greater than all of your fears and superstitions combined. It is the power to take possession of your own mind and direct it to whatever ends you may desire . . . When you speak of your poverty and lack of education,' Mr. Carnegie explained, 'you are simply directing your mind power to attract these undesirable circumstances because it is true that whatever your mind feeds upon, your mind attracts to you. Now you see why it is important that you recognize that all success begins with definiteness of purpose, with a clear picture in your mind of precisely what you want from life.'

Then Mr. Carnegie continued his speech with a description of a great universal truth which made such an impact upon my mind that I began then and there to give myself a new outlook on life and set up for myself a goal so far above my previous achievements that it shocked my friends and relatives when they heard about it. 'Everyone,' said Mr. Carnegie 'comes to the earth plane blessed with the privilege of controlling one's mind power and directing it to whatever end one may choose. But everyone brings over with oneself at birth, the equivalent of two sealed envelopes, one of which is clearly labeled The Riches You May Enjoy If You Take Possession of Your Own Mind and Direct It to Ends of Your Own Choice, and the other is labeled Penalties You Must Pay If You Neglect to Take Possession of Your Own Mind and Direct It.'[34]

Zenith concluded, "Hill's language can be a little outdated, but you get the gist."

"I hear what you're saying, and it sounds incredibly convincing but . . ." Skyler trailed off.

"But?" Zenith inquired drawing Skyler's concerns out of him.

"But one thing that's still bothering me is that I know that at the end of the day, not everyone is going to be wealthy," he said in genuine bewilderment.

"This is true!" Zenith agreed. "There is no doubt in my mind that not everyone is going to be wealthy, but it is also true that not everyone has recurring dreams of receiving $40 million. Listen," Zenith said as she tried to clarify her thoughts, "in one sense this dream has nothing to do with the money that you will make in the process of following your dreams. The $40 million is merely symbolic of you attaining as a free gift what now seems impossible to you. As Paulo Coelho says, 'It's the possibility of having a dream come true that makes life interesting.'"[35]

She went on, noticeably calming her passionate tone and slowing her pace. "Listen Skyler, I'm going to get psychological with you here for a minute so bear with me."

"Ok," he shrugged.

She continued, "Anyone can actualize their impossible dream if, in the sleeping hours when the defenses are down, one lets the enormous nature of one's dreams go wild with the intention of letting this love affair seep into and dominate the waking hours of existence when all of one's defenses tend to be up. This dream keeps coming to you while you're sleeping to show you one of your deepest desires while enticing you to reach for it. The defense mechanisms of the daytime usually remain on guard against such public displays of affection, which are seeking to repress one who is infatuated with the desire to love and live one's dream. This is nature's way of protecting each of us from the emotional pain that comes from expressing our unique individuality. It's also nature's way of cushioning us from the pain that comes from the possibility of failure. However, Skyler, through persistence to a clear vision, every dreamer comes to understand that no matter how unlikely, taboo or youthful these dreams may appear to be, the belly of the earth can and will still stretch with the conception of the new dream as sure as the belly of a woman can and will stretch with the conception of new life."

"Honey, this dream that you have had is about you becoming the person that you know deep down in the sleeping psyche of your subconscious mind that you are capable of becoming but which is now beyond your current conscious levels of belief. That is why this message keeps coming to you in a dream when your daytime defenses are pinned down; silent and unable wrestle against the wisdom of your deepest self. Your infinite self is showing up and showing out with a monstrous message for you about your genius and your inner power that you have been neglecting. As I like to say, 'Obscure dreams have so much to teach you about success, but you keep passing by the deserted wilderness of your mind for a more suitable address.' Skyler forget about the money if that is a distraction to you. Do it and pursue it for the neglected child prodigy within you that you will give new life to and unleash on the world in the process of following your dreams. Frank McCourt says, 'You might be poor, your shoes might be broken, but your mind is a palace,'[36] and since your mind is a palace, my love, it is time for you to live into the royal nature of it."

Zenith went on, "One of the greatest books ever written about following your dreams is the story of *The Alchemist*. It's about a young shepherd boy in Spain who leaves his life behind to follow his dreams of traveling the world in search of his treasure. That story did not resonate with millions of people all over the world and set the Guinness World Record for the most translated book by any living author because everyone who reads it thinks that they are going to travel to Egypt and find their own treasure there. The story is so meaningful because it reminds us all of the mystery and intrigue of our own personal dreams, or what *The Alchemist* calls, our own 'personal legend', which may seem impossible to us now, but that we must learn to follow to the fulfillment of our own personal potential."

"Skyler, your dream is not about everyone becoming wealthy," Zenith reiterated. "Everyone else has their own 'impossible dreams,' their own internal treasures to discover and their own personal blocks that they too must learn to master. But your internal desires have brought this specific dream to you and only you can master it. As Florence Scovel Shinn says, 'There is a place that you are to fill and no one else can fill, something you are to do, which no one else can do. There is a perfect picture of this in the super-conscious mind. It usually flashes across the consciousness as an unattainable ideal, something too good to be true. In reality it is one's true destiny or destination flashed to oneself from the infinite intelligence which is within oneself.'"[37]

Skyler didn't know how he had brought this dream to himself and he still wasn't sure that he could in fact become the master of his fate. But mystified as he was that this woman mysteriously knew the contents of his dream, he reasoned that maybe she had other inside knowledge that could even rectify his current inabilities. Although he wouldn't let it show, there was a tiny little glimmer of a *what-if* pinballing throughout his being and lighting up his consciousness with the most miniscule thought that wondered and mused, *"Just maybe!"* Maybe this lady could teach him how to master the game of life. He didn't know for sure, but one thing he knew for certain was that he wanted to hear more from her, especially her interpretation of his outrageous vision that had become so torturous to him.

6 SIGNS OF SELF WORTH

After Skyler had what appeared to be a sufficient amount of time to contemplate what she was saying, Zenith went on. "Now, concerning the other side of your internal dialogue, you know, the hunch that said that maybe this dream was given to you so that you could experience what it felt like to be valued and appreciated at the highest level? Well, this idea is compatible with the foretelling of a great-things-to-come interpretation of your dream. It does not have to be contradictory unless you choose to make it contradictory. Even with everything that we've previously discussed concerning believing in the impossible until it becomes an impossible possibility, the universe was, as you wisely suspected, also giving you a dream about your infinite self worth."

"Have you ever come across *Acres of Diamonds*?" Zenith asked.

"If I had, I'm pretty sure we wouldn't be here discussing all of this right now, would we?" Skyler said looking noticeably confused.

"No, no, no, crazy! I'm not talking about a field of physical diamonds," Zenith said, laughing while playfully waving away Skyler's confusion. "I'm talking about the story called *Acres of Diamonds.*"

"Nope, can't say that I've ever stumbled on that either," Skyler said.

"It is one of the most beautiful stories ever written about self worth, introduced to the world by Russell H. Conwell. It all revolves around a wealthy farmer in the Middle East named Ali Hafed. Ali Hafed was, we're told, 'contented because he was wealthy and wealthy because he was contented.'[38] As the story goes, one day an old wise man visits the farmer, and after telling Ali Hafed how diamonds were first created from sunlight, the wise man goes on to tell Ali Hafed how finding these diamonds could make him so wealthy that he and his children could become great rulers of lands both near and far."

"Conwell tells us that Ali Hafed went to bed a poor man that evening. 'Poor because he was discontented and discontented because he thought that he was poor.'[39] Well, since the man was so set on traveling for his diamonds, he sold his farm and left his family with a neighbor in order to journey far and wide in search of every mountain range that cradled the diamonds in the white sands beneath them. Ali Hafed began at the base of the mountains that surrounded his town with no luck. Next, he went to Palestine, also unsuccessfully. He finally he traveled all throughout Europe where he lost all of his money and ended his journey broken and destitute looking out on the Bay of Barcelona in Spain. There, he threw himself into the tide, which swept him under the water to his tragic and unfortunate destiny. However, this tragedy is not where the story ends."

Zenith continued, "One day, the man who had moved into Ali Hafed's house stumbled upon a black stone that reflected many different colors while taking care of his animals in the stream out back. Not thinking much of it, he took it inside and set it on the shelf above the fireplace. A few days later, the old wise man visited, and to his absolute astonishment beheld one of the finest diamonds that he had ever seen. In the wise man's excitement, he asked if Ali Hafed had returned. The owner said that Ali Hafed had not returned and that it was no diamond but just a simple rock that he had found behind Ali Hafed's house. However, the wise man insisted that it was indeed a diamond. With great anticipation the two men returned to the stream and uncovered the most magnificent diamond mine of all time beneath the white sands in the stream right there on Ali Hafed's property. The story concludes by saying, 'Had Ali Hafed remained at home and dug in his own garden . . . he would have had acres of diamonds.'"[40]

"That is quite a story," Skyler said in a quiet voice while looking down, obviously shaken by the plight of Ali Hafed. It was as if there was a puppet master within Skyler's heart who tugged at the heartstrings of his internal shame, which was also connected to his facial expressions. It was this unknown force within Skyler that made him unable to look up at Zenith with the same comfort and confidence that had connected them as friends and confidants throughout the night. Shifting from pain to angst, Skyler became a simmering cauldron slightly spitting the boiling contents of his unsurfaced emotions as he slowly said, "I want to say that I don't understand how the wise man could be considered wise for sending Ali Hafed on a wild goose chase." Then his tone retracted as it was reeled back into melancholy and Skyler continued, "But that's no good because there's no way that the wise man could have known that there were diamonds behind Ali Hafed's house."

Here Zenith, mirrored his quiet tone saying, "Yes, my dear. And in a way, the story is not about the wise man nor is it particularly about Ali Hafed either. To take it a step further, the story is not even about Ali Hafed's unluckiness nor is it about his successor's supposed luckiness for being in the right place at the right time. As I see it, the story is about searching outside of ourselves when each of us is already rich with the true wealth that is inherently ours at birth and beyond it."

Skyler shifted awkwardly in his seat a bit then asked, "What do you mean by implying that we are wealthy even prior to our birth?"

Zenith replied, "Well, my love, there is no new energy in this universe, right?"

"That's true," Skyler said pensively.

"So, if you exist now in any physical form, you were already a part of this universe in some other form of energy even before you arrived in the state that we now know as you. If you are any form of energy at all, even prior to birth, you were already cast in the greatest show in the universe. Do you know the name of the show that I speak of, my dear?"

Skyler shrugged as he tentatively ventured out on a limb, "I guess it would be called *Existence* or something of that nature?"

"Exactly, my love! Only the best stars, moons, suns, trees, things, animals, planets and people with the perfect energy for this production make what I call *The Big Show*. The show has a limitless budget and it's the highest grossing show ever made. There will be no new cast members. Everything and everyone that is here has always been and will always be here as the final cut and chosen cast in the greatest story ever told. Welcome to *Existence*!

You made the final cut and you can never be cut, my love. You'll dance on earth's stage in this earth suit for now and then you'll remove this costume and your energy will continue to dance and perform in different costumes just as it has always done before you donned this one."

Zenith went on, "I once saw a bumper sticker that read 'Live like you have a backstage pass.'[41] Most people live like there isn't enough space for them to live out the expansiveness of who they really are. They hide and play small as if their being here were some kind of a mistake. But this bumper sticker made me think to myself that it's easy to 'Live like you have a backstage pass,' once you experientially know that you yourself have been cast as the star of the show. It's ironic that we aim for the stars, but many shooting stars kill themselves just to catch a dying glimpse of the radiant face of humanity. It's like we're shooting for the stars when those unattainable stars are shooting for the dazzling brilliance of everything that we are."

"You are so infinitely valuable that the greatest show in the universe literally could not and will never exist without your energy; without you. As the mystical poet named Rumi writes, 'You are not [just] a drop in the ocean. You are the entire ocean in a [single] drop.'[42] Regardless of what you choose to do with your energy, the universe could not be more delighted with you, and for that reason, it keeps the lights bright, the cameras focused, and action rolling to capture the fullness of the part that you play, captivated by the magnificence of your valuable contribution to the universe."

"My story is filled with so many holes that it doesn't seem like much of a contribution at all!" Skyler firmly asserted, voicing his doubts.

"Yes, my dear! We all deal with those feelings from time to time. But what you must always remember is that one of the greatest paths to wholeness is learning how to accept the holes," Zenith said with a knowing and compassionate smile.

She went on, "Spiritual teacher Lao Tzu says, 'We join spokes together in a wheel, but it is the center hole that makes the wagon move. We shape clay into a pot, but it is the emptiness inside that holds whatever we want. We hammer wood for a house, but it is the inner space that makes it livable. We work with being, but non-being is what we use.'"[43]

Wrinkling his eyebrows and rubbing his temple and forehead with his fingers as if this would magically connect the dots of his memories, Skyler replied as if musing to himself, "That sounds strangely familiar. Where have I heard that before?"

After a few moments, being that he was unable to recall the connection, Zenith lifted a questioning eyebrow, shrugged and went on, "Do you understand what all of this means, my dear?"

"I'm pretty sure that it has something to do with acceptance as you've said, but it's still a bit vague to me," Skyler replied.

"Basically, what I'm saying is this. Just as we often focus on the cup for containing the contents that we want to consume, but it is actually the emptiness inside of the cup that makes space to hold our heart's desire, the emptiness or the 'holes' as you put it— that we often experience in life are just as important as the times that we feel filled with life and happiness."

Zenith continued, "Think about it. Whose side of the story made *Acres of Diamonds* more powerful, Ali Hafed's tragic side or the part that was played by the fortunate man who moved into his house?"

Skyler responded, "I want to say Ali Hafed, but it seems so wrong. I mean, earlier I was so repulsed by his unlucky fate in the story. But now I see that without him there would be no story. I mean the plot surely wouldn't be anything worth remembering without him. And yet, without Ali Hafed's successor, there would be no moral to the story. It would still be incomplete. That's mindboggling now that I think about it."

Zenith replied, "Yes, my dear, it's just as the old saying goes, 'The sun sacrifices its pride to the guillotine of the night, realizing darker perspectives can often be just as bright.' Welcome to the Yin and Yang—dual nature of existence. There is no day that does not touch and leak into the night, there is no bad that does not touch and mingle with the good, there is no storm that does not in some way renew and ultimately replenish the earth. This is a picture of radical acceptance but as Byron Katie, the author of the book *Loving What Is* says, 'There's nothing that we can do that doesn't help the planet. That's the way it really is.'[44] In the end there is no duality there is only oneness. Love remains balanced at the center of the seesaw of all life. As extremities of the center of the seesaw, we may ascend or descend but we remain connected to the center. The center would not be the center unless it remained just as close to one extremity of life as it does to the other. The light is not superior to the darkness, there's only love that sees infinite value everywhere, which undergirds and supports both extremes of life where everything and everyone plays their part. And every part works together for the good of the whole; the good of the one epic performance of *Existence*."

Zenith continued, "There's absolutely nothing in all creation that can ever separate you from what Paulo Coelho calls 'the soul of the universe,'[45] or the love of your infinite inner being. So, the dream keeps coming to you in order to tell you that you are wealthy beyond your wildest imaginations of wealth just like Ali Hafed was. Had Ali Hafed decided not to take his life and rather returned home like the prodigal son to his true nature and his infinite self worth, he would have found that it was his negative and unsuccessful journey that positively led him to his own inner treasure, which was his all along. He would have found as someone wisely stated that, 'Sometimes the wrong choices bring us to the right places.'[46] And he would have to admit, as I love to say that 'Sometimes the things that destroy you become the architectural blueprints which make your mind royal.'"

Zenith went on, "Do you see the irony of it all? Not only was Ali Hafed already wealthy with money, contentment and relationships, but he was also sitting on a previously undiscovered diamond mine of his own unique dance with destiny. Meanwhile, Ali Hafed is traveling the whole world over searching outside of his own property, outside of his own self and outside of his own experience for the wealth that he unknowingly already has at home. He refuses to treasure himself above all else and so he perceives himself—the richest man in the world—to be utterly poor and needy. Each one of us is potentially Ali Hafed to the extent that we lose sight of our infinite self worth that is our own unique energy and contribution to the universe. We are all potentially Ali Hafed's successor to the extent that we cultivate our own crops and discover and mine our own diamond *mind* within. When we do that, as I love to say, 'We will open up to our vast potential and impregnate the world with a river of diamonds.'"

At this point, Skyler replied, "I'm getting a better grasp of what you're saying but all of this talk about Ali Hafed leaving what he had in order to search outside does make me wonder if I should have just stayed at my first job from the very beginning?"

To this, Zenith replied, "Honey, infinite self worth isn't about staying in a job that you hate, nor is it about leaving it for that matter. As you will soon see, your dream is communicating some pretty radical permission for you to begin a new life as you see fit. Infinite self worth is not something that you can lose or ever be separated from regardless of the decisions that you make in life to go right or to go left."

"It's about finally coming to the experiential knowledge of choosing yourself after you have spent your whole life choosing everything but yourself. This is why Howard Thurman says, 'Don't ask what the world needs. Ask what makes you come alive and go do it. Because what the world needs is people who have come alive.'[47] Choosing yourself is the narrow path that leads to life, which most people miss as they focus on what's to the right of them or what's to the left of them. Both of these options are just outside of the narrow gate of the truest self that leads to the true inner wealth."

"Infinite self worth is more than discovering that you are wearing some invisible crown. It is awakening out of a state of amnesia to find that you yourself are the kingly creator of your existence. What does it matter if the king chooses to go this way or that? To travel or to stay put? When all is said and done, you are still the king. This kingly or queenly consciousness is what I meant earlier when I said that most people have never even met the true nature of themselves. Had Ali Hafed known who he really was, he would have known that whether he traveled or stayed at home that he was already royalty and that he was loaded with both discovered and undiscovered treasures."

"Often, after making a major life-change such as quitting a job or leaving a relationship that no longer fits us nor defines us anymore, we have these dreadful 'Oh shit!' moments that make us wonder if we just made the stupidest decision of our lives. Were we following some misleading pipe dream? Can our hearts be trusted? What if we fail and betray ourselves, betray our families and betray everything that we've worked so hard to establish? Do we amount to much, and are there really diamonds that can be mined from the depths of ourselves when we are placed under the pressure to perform? Can I actually do what I thought I could do? These are the kind of questions that can boggle our minds in these dreadful 'What have I done?' moments."

"But you, sweet genius, were not misleading yourself for daring to believe in the magic that has been conceived by the infinite intelligence inside of you. In the case of this dream, just after leaving the life that you'd worked so hard to establish for many years, your infinite self was and still is showing up to you in the form of this dream to say in effect, 'You are infinitely worth more than you can imagine. Don't give up on yourself and everything that caused you to leave your old life behind. It is time to receive and richly reward yourself with the infinite value that has been locked deep within yourself and deep within your heart. As Joseph Campbell says, 'The cave you fear to enter holds the treasure that you seek.'[48] Your heart is that cave and it's time to enter that cave now! You are like the boy in *The Alchemist* seeking his treasure and Dorothy in Oz seeking a way home, who both already had infinite worth and everything that they desired inside of them before they ever left in search of it. But if they never went on their costly journeys outside, they never would have found their way to the free treasures within. The things you feel deep inside are trustworthy guides. Everything is right on time and you are going to be just fine.'"

"In other words, the dream was communicating both financial stability and a message of deep self worth wrapped up in one unforgettable vision. Your dream is about so much more than receiving wealth. It is about receiving and living into your internal value. But external wealth should not be discounted because internal value often amplifies external wealth. Florence Scovel Shinn demonstrates this concept in a beautiful story when she writes:

> *Wealth is a matter of consciousness. The French have a legend giving an example of this. A poor man was walking along a road when he met a traveler. He stopped him and said, 'My good friend, I see you are poor. Take this gold nugget, sell it and you will be rich all your days.' The man was overjoyed at his good fortune and he took the nugget home. He immediately found work and he became so prosperous that he did not sell the nugget. Years passed and he became a very rich man.*
>
> *One day he met a poor man on the road. He stopped him and said, 'My good friend, I will give you this gold nugget, which if you sell will make you rich for life.' The mendicant took the nugget, had it valued and found that it was only brass. So, we see the first man became rich through feeling rich, thinking the nugget was gold. Everyone has within them a gold nugget. It's one's consciousness of gold, of opulence, that brings riches into one's life.[49]*

"Sounds to me like someone pulled a fast one on the first man!" Skyler said to Zenith with a wide-eyed grin.

"Exactly, my friend!" Zenith said before continuing, "Sometimes we must trick the mind, until it believes that it's really doing magic when it's simply operating according to its original intentions and internal designs."

"Sounds about right," Skyler agreed before continuing. "And that story kind of reminds me of the old proverb that says, 'Sometimes we need a wise guide to peel back the ceiling of our lives to remind us that infinity never places any limits on our skies.'"

"That's one of my favorites!" Zenith replied. "Anyway, earlier you said that your dream made you feel for the first time that you had gotten paid what you were worth. Well, darling, you're worth much more than $40 million and my hope is that by the end of tonight that you'll have a deeply rooted experiential knowledge of your infinite self worth and that you won't need a dream, anything, nor anyone else to know and feel that feeling ever again.

To this Skyler replied, "Even though there's still so much that I have to learn, I feel like I'm actually starting to get this stuff, and it's beginning to sink in . . . even if a bit slowly."

Zenith nodded knowingly, then concluded by saying, "As promised, now that we've laid a solid foundation, I want to get into the long-awaited interpretation of your dream by introducing you to the characters in it beginning with the man who died."

Skyler never recognized any of the faces of the people in his reoccurring dream and didn't even think that he'd be familiar with them if they walked in the front door at that very moment. Since their personal identities had already receded to the background of his mind, he chalked them up as faceless extras in the scenes of his dream even though each of them had played major roles in it.

He never expected to find out who the characters in this mysterious dream were. But now, he wondered who or what within his present or future life, the man who died, the two men bearing the envelopes and the woman who had received the twin check for $40 million might represent. What important truths might they have been trying to communicate? Although he had been with Zenith for what must have been hours now, this was the moment that he had been waiting for. If he had to be honest with himself, he'd have to admit that other than being undeniably enchanted by Zenith and her beauty, this was the only reason that he had ever entered the coffee shop in the first place.

7 THE FIVE CHARACTERS AND WHAT THEY REPRESENT

I
THE MAN WHO DIED

After making them both a fresh cup of coffee, Zenith began once again, "This dream took place in the office that you had just resigned from in real life. It's always important to take note of the locations in which your dreams take place because they can be massive indicators of the purpose and meaning of the dream itself. I once heard of a movie scriptwriter that had a dream that he was running away from someone who was chasing him until finally, they'd both arrived at the house that the scriptwriter had grown up in and the pursuit continued into the house. The scriptwriter who was telling the story said that he ran up the stairs and down the hall to his room. Just as he was about to slam the door behind him in order to barricade himself in his room, he turned to get a good look at the person that was pursuing him."

"To his utter astonishment, when he turned to face his assailant, his whole body swelled up with muscles that he didn't even know that he had, blades came out of his hands like the Wolverine from the comic series *X-Men* and he was no longer afraid, but he actually felt sorry for the intruder because he instinctively knew that this intruder was about to be thrashed by the person, or by the 'Wolverine' that the dreamer had now become. In real life, the scriptwriter had just finished writing his first script and feared what others might think about it. However, the childhood location of the dream, which was where he'd grown up and his action in the dream, which revolved around facing his fears, signified that this was a dream about growing up and facing his fears."

"When he faced his fears in the dream, a previously undiscovered power came out of his hands. This caused his whole body to mature and this power filled his mind with such courage and confidence that fear was forced to vacate the premises inside of him. The dream was indicating that by growing up and facing his fears, a power would come out of his hands, which was incredibly significant to him because he was a writer, and this power would cause him to live with a fearless maturity."

"As the African proverb says, 'If there is no fear within, the enemy without can do us no harm.'[50] The location and landscape of our dreams can help us understand and navigate the complex terrain of our psychological landscape as it pertains to the meaning of our dreams."

"Astonishing!" Skyler replied, "What an empowering dream!"

"It really is," Zenith said before continuing. "The scriptwriter went on to produce some of the greatest stories ever told, but he credits much of his success to his willingness to follow the maturity-dream that first taught him the importance of focusing on his work and forgetting what others thought about it."

Returning again to the interpretation of Skyler's personal dream, Zenith said, "Again, the dream where you received a fortune, took place in the office that you had just resigned from in real life. This resignation was a kind of death in that it signified your final departure from a life of which you had spent many hard-working adulthood years building, but could no longer live now that you'd decided to leave it all behind. Jungian Psychologist James Hollis teaches that a midlife crisis does not have to be a crisis but more of a rite of passage as we learn to let go of the masks, illusions and facades that fall away and die simply because we no longer have the energy to uphold them anymore.[51] A 'crisis' during midlife only occurs if we fail to make peace with this normal and natural process of death and maturity."

Skyler snickered, "I'm pretty sure I missed that boat that the psychologist was floating on because my life has definitely spiraled into a crisis."

Zenith laughed and said, "Well sweetheart, you don't know what you don't know, and when you do know how to be the captain of your own fate, a custom-made boat will be designed and delivered just for you. It took the novelist Sue Monk Kidd six years to finally finish her first novel called *The Secret Life of Bees*, after starting it and promptly shelving it six years prior. In that sixth year she was visiting the ancient Greek city of Ephesus with her daughter on a post graduation trip and prayed for guidance, in a historical olive grove chapel, asking about whether she should continue writing the novel or quit. When she went outside right after asking for a sign, a bee landed on her shoulder and stayed there as her and her daughter walked all the way back to the tour bus. Initially, her daughter tried to shoo it away, but Sue stopped her, knowing that this was the bee that had been sent to her in response to her asking for guidance just a few moments earlier. In her book *E-Cubed* a sequel to her best-selling book *E-Squared*, Pam Grout says this about Sue Monk Kidd's encounter with the bee that forever changed her life:

> *Once you find out about the power of your thoughts and consciousness, there is no turning back. You can't really undrink the Kool-Aid.*
>
> *You can choose not to use this information, you can be like Cypher in The Matrix, who told Morpheus to shove that red pill right up his ass, but you can never forget. And, in fact, you can never "not use" it. You just do it unconsciously, creating your life with society's default setting, reinforcing the historical tale of woe.*
>
> *Where our story departs Hollywood is that in real life, you get unlimited chances to choose the red pill. Opportunities, like whiskers, keep coming back.*
>
> *People mistakenly worry there's a time limit for their good, a sell-by date. They fret that they missed their chance back in 1986 or that time they turned down so-and-so. The chance to create your good reappears over and over every moment. You can't really miss the boat because there's another one right behind it.*[52]

Skyler nodded with understanding signaling that he was picking up what Zenith was putting down and she went on, "When you received this dream, in real life, you could no longer go on living by the same standards that once gave your life meaning. This is why you had been so dead-set on resigning in the first place. The shell of your old life didn't fit you anymore and was ready to be discarded. So, the psychological landscape of the dream was resignation, death and permission to proceed into your new life. Of course, this means that the man who died in the dream was actually you, or better said, the man who died was the person that you used to be."

"Woah! I definitely didn't see that coming," Skyler responded with a stunned expression on his face before continuing with more questions. "Wait? I am the man who died in the dream. How's that possible when I was alive and represented by my normal self in the dream?"

"Bear with me, tiger!" Zenith said smiling. "It will all make more sense as we proceed, but for now just know that this among other things was a resignation-dream that communicated that your old life was dead and that you are now free to journey on into your new life. That someone, who finally recognized your value, was your old self and this is why you had the courage to leave a job that no longer fit the person you were evolving into in the first place. But, once recognized, a kind of death was necessary in order to cocoon and reinvent yourself into the newly recognized state of existence."

"I'm absolutely mind-blown right now!" Skyler admitted as he gestured with his hand like a gun to his head.

Zenith advanced, "There is no outside source nor force to recognize our work or our worth like the deepest self within us. Our deepest self sees all, knows all and rewards us richly. This self is the one that is fully loaded with treasures and still had so much to give, even in death. It would be foolish for you, or anyone else for that matter, as you transitioned from one stage of life to the next, to throw out every part of your old life just because you have evolved and become someone new. Through this dream, your deepest self was signifying that although your former self had died, it was passing its infinite wealth and treasures on to your new self."

Amazed, reanimated and looking with new eyes at the dream that had become a nightmare to him, Skyler pondered, "That is crazy deep!"

"You are crazy deep and you're just beginning to scratch the surface of it all," Zenith shot back. "Before I move on to introduce you to the woman in your dream, I want to share a story with you called *The Wise Man and The Beggar* told by spiritual teacher Eckhart Tolle."

"I'm all ears," Skyler replied.

Zenith resumed, "In it, a beggar asks a man on the street for some spare change. The man replies that he doesn't have any money, but asks what the beggar is sitting on. The beggar says, 'Oh that's nothing, just an old box that I've been sitting on for years.' 'Ever look inside?' the wise man inquires as he urges the beggar to look inside. When the man opens the box, he is astonished to find a load of pure gold coins that come tumbling out in an avalanche from within. Eckhart Tolle goes on to say that his teaching is about getting you to find that treasure that comes from looking inside.[53] As I like to say, 'Many pirates passionately sail from place to place seeking other people's possessions, never stopping to ponder that their rib cage might ultimately be their most radiantly valuable treasure chest.'"

Skyler liked these sayings but something about them perplexed him. So, he said, "I can vividly see exactly what you're saying but I just don't know how to do it. How do you look within and get the treasures out?"

"Great question!" Zenith said. "Just keep it simple, love. Your treasure is symbolic of anything you really desire that now seems unattainable to you in your present situation. In the story of *The Alchemist* that I spoke of earlier, the young shepherd boy in Spain had a dream, which signified that if he traveled to the Egyptian pyramids, he would indeed find a buried treasure there just for him. When the boy awoke, he was electrified by his dream and electrified with new possibility."

"The Danish philosopher Soren Kierkegaard says, and I'm paraphrasing here, but when 'someone has grown faint about the silent despair they have been living in, the water that they most need someone to fetch for them is the refreshing water of new possibility because sipping it or being splashed by it can magically snap anyone out of the stupor of a depressing life.'[54] The dream that the shepherd boy in the Alchemist had was this needed possibility that both quenched a deep thirst in the boy and simultaneously awakened an even greater one. However, through years of natural pre-programming, when he fully awoke from his dream and began to think about his profession and giving up his sheep, he quickly dissuaded himself from any chances of stepping off the ledge of his comfort zone with the strong and capable wings of his new dream."

"Nevertheless, by some twist of fate, the boy bumped into an old sage while walking through the town the next day. The wise man tells the boy that he doesn't know if the boy will choose to journey under the guidance of the dream that he'd had, but if he goes to Egypt, he will surely find his treasure! The boy is astounded that this stranger could know such secrets. At the same time, he is also reanimated with hope for what the dream could signify about the larger world out there beyond the world that he was familiar with. He wanted to explore and adventure so badly, but if he was honest with himself, he had no clue where to begin. Any of this sound familiar?" Zenith asked rhetorically. Skyler nodded knitting his eyebrows comprehendingly and she continued. "After speaking further with the old man about dreams, desires and the nature of the world, the old man ultimately explains that, 'When you want something, all the universe conspires in helping you to achieve it.'"[55]

"Damn!" Skyler replied with goose bumps rising, "What an astounding thing to say to someone!"

"Yes, my dear it is a truly captivating concept. However, the power of these words will soon fade from your mind and their impact will lose their grip on you unless you see your own life as a sequel to this story."

Then Skyler replied pensively by saying, "That makes sense and I am assuming that the boy did eventually go in search of his treasure. But let me ask you this . . . What was it that finally convinced the boy that going all in on following his dream to seek his treasure was the right decision for him?"

"Well," Zenith answered "as he thought about his present life and everything that he would have to leave behind to pursue his future, for some reason the wind caught his attention and he began to ponder it and compare himself with it. The story goes on to say that, "The boy felt jealous of the winds and saw that he could have the same freedom (that the winds had). There was nothing to hold him back except himself."[56]

"Just like the boy in the story or coach Lou Holtz writing down his one hundred and seven impossible goals that he wanted to achieve before he died, in order to get your treasures out, you must first put your treasures in. You put your treasures in by fully accepting, embracing and clarifying the reality of your dream or the reality of what you want. Set an intention, a chief aim or a definite goal in your life and develop what Napoleon Hill calls 'an intense burning desire' that no amount of trials or mishaps can thwart or steer you away from. Then, once your internal guidance has been set, you move towards your outward goal never taking your eyes off of the pyramids or the place of your promised treasure. Meanwhile the science of unseen forces will be rearranging the universe and all of reality to come to your aid."

"This kind of unshakable persistence that you'll develop is key because the universe always bends reality and we too become capable of bending reality when we hold the vision of what we want with unbending intentions."

"Huh?" Skyler stalled, "You're going to have to run that by me again."

Zenith repeated her words slowly, "The universe always bends reality to our wish when we hold the vision of what we want with unbending intent. You bend reality to your wish when you hold the vision of what you want with unbending intent. Since your mind is magnetic, you will come to understand that where your presence is, your future will also be. As Bertice Berry says, 'When you walk with purpose you collide with destiny'[57] and as I love to say, 'You collide with destiny caught up in the awe and mystery of walking the halls of a mind that's only inclined to recognize and expect victory.'"

Zenith advanced, "There are no limits to what your internal desires can achieve because you are and were made to be an uncontainable cosmic force. However, you must always remember and accept that on this quest to create there may be a time of testing before you see your creation materialize. Paulo Coelho, the author of *The Alchemist* says that when he was young, his parents thought that he was so crazy for wanting to be a writer that they put him in a psychiatric institution. Their family had worked so hard to secure a good place in Brazilian society and they believed that being an aspiring writer was clearly throwing all of that away. Coelho broke out of the institution three times before later being released."

"However, in his early twenties Coelho wrote in his journal, 'Everyday it seems harder to achieve my great ideal, to be famous and respected, to be the man who wrote the book of the century, the thought of the millennium, the history of humanity.' Coelho admits that his parents were right in regard to the thought that he was a bit of a megalomaniac for writing these words and thinking this way long before he was ever even an author. But he also admits that it was his thinking big, rather than thinking small, which helped to create the reality that he now lives as the celebrated author that he had always dreamed of becoming."[58]

"I tell you this story so that you notice the patience that Coelho demonstrated on his quest to create. He didn't write *The Alchemist* until he was nearly forty years old and it would be years or even decades later before the book would receive all the notoriety that it has received today. Had Coelho quit when he was thirty-five years old, not only would he have never written *The Alchemist,* but he would have never known the thrill of having become one who transforms common things into gold himself."

"Many people quit during this time of testing. They take their challenges to mean that their goals must not be meant to be, rather than accepting these challenges as stepping-stones to cross every rushing river of obstacles to the realization of their dreams. But this deep existential acceptance of life with all of its uncertainties, challenges and hardships will give you a sense of invincible happiness along the path to your goal. As I like to say, 'One of the greatest keys to happiness is learning how to accept reality while stretching forth to create a new one.'"

Zenith continued, "You will come to discover that your own happiness is everything and it will be the undergirding life force that carries you on. 'Following your bliss,'[59] the phrase coined by Joseph Campbell, the professor of mythology whose writings inspired the making of *Star Wars*, provides the perfect image of attaining this happiness if you use the phrase properly. But if your bliss always remains one step ahead of you, then the unfortunate reality is that you cannot, and will never possess it. You must love your ideal self, as well as your real self, because if you're always waiting for your next ideal, you'll never get an opportunity to experience your own unconditional love of yourself at the level of the real. This is why I say that, 'One of the greatest keys to happiness is realizing it has no doors.' There are no necessary conditions, nor any prerequisites needed before you can enter into happiness. It is yours for the taking at any moment. Therefore, the best way to 'follow your bliss' is to experience the blissful happiness of internally achieving your goal on the way to externally receiving it."

"What do you mean by that?" Skyler inquired. "How can I experience the happiness of achieving my goal before I actually achieve my goal?"

"It seems like a contradiction, right!" Zenith agreed. "But nevertheless, it is indeed true, as the prolific author and energy experimenter extraordinaire Pam Grout makes overwhelmingly clear in her story about the uneducated cofounder of Twitter. Pam says:

Biz Stone who went from college drop out to wildly successful entrepreneur worth $250 Million saw his role at Twitter as being the non-worrier. When everything is wrong and broken, instead of harping on what's wrong and broken, find what works and build on that. He says the solution always emerges if you look for the positive. Biz throws around words like infinite possibilities. He knows attitude is everything and that we pull from the quantum field a match to our beliefs and expectations. As he says, for any one problem there are infinite potential solutions. Creativity he argues is limitless. If you cling to what you know, you miss out on the limitless possibilities.

When Biz was unemployed and living in his mom's basement, he printed business cards touting "Biz Stone, Genius". He claimed to be building inventions with infinite resources and a world-class team of scientists at his head quarters—naturally titled "Genius Labs". It was his pronouncement of this dream that brought it into reality. He knew to focus on the end result desired.

That same visualization launched his career at Google. He determined he wanted to work there and even though he had no college degree and Google typically restricts their employee searches to PhD's, he visualized his way in. He says he saw it clearly in his mind's eye before it came true. "I'd manufactured this opportunity without a college education much less a higher degree, without working my way up a ladder. I wasn't a shoo-in. I wasn't anything. But I did have experience in one particular area: Creating my own opportunities." As he says, "Hard work is

> *important, but success is more about looking through*
> *the lens of infinite possibility."[60]*

Coming to the point of her story she said, "So do you see now, how you can experience the happiness of achieving your goal before you actually achieve it? It all revolves around the intention of visualizing life the way you want it to be through the power of your imagination and experiencing the exhilaration of the new reality that you are focusing on. This is why I told you earlier to remember and to pack your filter with the thrilling feelings of the dream that you were given. It all centers on the science that your universe is being made in your image, in your likeness and in the exact replica of your mind."

"That's magical," Skyler said, as if deep in contemplation.

Everything that Zenith was saying and the stories that she told him, were beginning to crystalize in his mind as the simplicity of it all started to settle on him with a new warmth of understanding. It was a crazy feeling, but it felt like the universe had its hands busy in her mind, knitting words together to blanket his heavy heart with something intricately designed.

He then replied, "In other words what your saying is, I can use my past feelings of excitement at good things in my dreams and my feelings of satisfaction from other things that I have already received to build a present paradise of emotions that perpetuate themselves in the out-picturing of my future?"

Zenith stared at Skyler in amazement with her mouth agape and replied with a slight smile in a voice that was so quiet that it was almost inaudible, "Yes, my love. Exactly. That's genius and certainly more brilliant than I've ever stated it! I like how you said to 'build a present paradise of emotions because they will perpetuate themselves in your future.' The truth is that whether we build a paradise of emotions or see and attach to the feelings of a paradise lost, we will project that reality into our future. That is why I always say, 'What we perceive always determines the reality that we perpetuate,' and that is why it is so important to master your moods, your internal dialogue and your internal vision and concept of yourself. Neville Goddard even takes this discussion of mastering your mentality a step further and says, 'Create a scene in your mind's eye and believe its reality into being. That invisible state will produce the objective state you desire. For all objective reality is solely produced by imagination.'"[61]

Zenith advanced further, "This is not about forcing the outer world to change, it's simply about feeling deeply within that things are the way we imagine them to be. As Jim Kwik says, 'If an egg is broken by outside force, Life ends. If broken by inside force, Life begins. Great things always begin from inside.'[62] Although Skyler immediately saw himself in this quote, his focus was not on the depressing and devastating thought of himself as the egg falling from bridge. Rather, his mind was wondering how to inwardly focus his attention on great things for himself, because he realized now that he wanted life to begin again for him. He also realized that just thinking about this brought him a touch of happiness that was beginning to thaw the glacier within him that his heart had somehow become.

Zenith continued on, "No, you cannot force the outside world to change. As I like to say, 'There is a medical condition for people who are constantly trying to force shit to happen.'"

"What's that?" Skyler asked.

"It's called hemorrhoids!" Zenith said this with such a straight face and such an intense gaze at Skyler that he couldn't help but begin laughing hysterically. This was the desired effect and Zenith cracked up as well. After catching his breath, Skyler said, "Wait a minute. You're not a doctor. Did you learn that from personal experience?" To which Zenith sheepishly replied, "Maybe. Well, kind of!" This killed Skyler and as if her comment had shot him in the nose, he immediately snorted as even more laughter came oozing out.

The snort however only triggered Zenith even further, and leaning back in her chair from the gut-wrenching laugher, she lost control, her arms started flailing and she fell flat on her back, which in turn only produced even more laughter from the both of them. It was quite a scene, and as he picked himself up from off of the floor and he helped her up, Skyler realized that he hadn't had this much fun in an incredibly long time. He also realized that in the same way that all of their laughter had brought both of them to the ground, the change in atmosphere had made large portions of the glacier around his heart come crashing down inside of him, which was why he was now experiencing genuine happiness that he didn't want to end.

After gathering their composure and moving from the table to the couch area with a pitcher of ice cold water, Zenith said, "Now that we have discussed the man who died in your dream, I think you're ready for me to introduce you to the woman in your dream who, in her own unique way, will more thoroughly reiterate the simplicity of radiating a new reality in order for you to mine the treasures that you seek within." To this Skyler nodded as Zenith took a sip of water from her glass before proceeding.

II
THE WOMAN

"Now, here's where things get really juicy!" Zenith said with a cunning smile. Skyler just shrugged, wrinkled his eyebrows having no idea what to expect and said, "Ok." Zenith began, "It would be easy to guess that the woman in your dream, who also received a check that was a twin to yours, was symbolic of a business partner or a romantic partner who would naturally be receiving a perfect split of your dreams come true. In this case, correct me if I'm wrong, your wife does have complete access to everything good that comes to you just as you also share in everything that comes to her?" Skyler nodded briefly and Zenith continued. "However, this is not the interpretation of the dream. The woman in this dream is symbolic of the higher feminine consciousness of your intuitive self."

"Hold on!" Skyler interjected, "Are you saying that my highest self is a chick?"

Laughing out loud, Zenith went on, "Don't go getting all self-conscious and butthurt, sweetheart. I'm saying that the woman in your dream is symbolic of living by instinct and I'm saying that this dream happens to be all about you. Through the years, intuition has been socially symbolized as a female characteristic, and although this interpretation serves humanity well, there is still more to understand. However, dreams have a short amount of time to capture our attention with relatable symbols that we can understand, and it seems that the universe has obviously used something witty enough to capture your attention on this one," Zenith said as she flashed her eyebrows and snickered.

"Intuition is defined as, 'The ability to understand something instinctively, without the need for conscious reasoning'[63] and is also defined as, 'a thing that one knows or considers likely from instinctive feeling rather than conscious reasoning.'[64] In contrast with the character personified as yourself in the dream, who had no clue who'd died nor why that person had left you an envelope, the woman in the dream *knew* the man who'd died. Knowing the man who'd died, she also knew that he was incredibly wealthy and she had no doubt that she would be a recipient of a massive portion of that wealth."

Zenith went on, "Whether the man who died had previously told her about her inheritance or not was of no importance. Many people are told of great expectations however, they still fail to live expectantly. To live in eager expectation is to live in the full consciousness of our realized desire or to live in the consciousness of accomplishment. When we live in this state, we know that it's already done, that nothing can stop it, that failure is impossible and future success is inevitable. This certainty permeates everything that we do because we have already experienced the reality of our vision so vividly in our mind that we know intrinsically with every fiber of our being that the hands of the universe are shaping a new reality according to and in unison with the hands of our wish."

"The important thing about this woman is what she believed. Or to be more precise, the important thing about this woman is what *she knew*. And what did she know? What she said in the dream was that she *knew* that the man who had died was loaded and that she was going to be financially set for life."

"I see," Skyler pondered as if he was deep in thought.

Zenith replied, "Yes, you can now see that in answer to your question about mining your treasures within and getting those treasures out, the woman in your dream makes it so simple."

Excitedly, Skyler cut in, "I simply need to know that I am capable of anything. I set my mind on the treasure that I want, either financially, relationally, emotionally or otherwise and I hold to the vision that the contents of my mind will be brewed into my life, to use your earlier analogy?"

"Precisely!" Zenith exclaimed. "Know what you want. Imagine what it would look like and feel like to have it, be it and experience it. Then hold to and affirm the images of that reality and radiate the feelings of that reality until the old reality melts away and the new reality presents itself in your world as it has for every 'alchemist' that we have spoken of tonight and countless others that have gone unmentioned."

"If you have ever experienced the feminine beauty and elegance of human intuition, you know that it is as equally powerful as it is alluring. However, as mentioned earlier, you don't have to be a woman to embrace this quality in yourself. You simply have to be willing to follow your deepest feelings rather than waiting to act until you have everything perfectly reasoned out. When it comes to embracing the duality of the masculine and feminine aspects of ourselves, we should be like the mystical poet Hafiz who tells a story that illustrates this balance with wisdom and love. Hafiz states,

> *Once a young woman asked me, 'How does it feel to be a man?' And I replied, 'My dear, I am not so sure.' Then she said, 'Well, aren't you a man?' And this time I replied, 'I view gender as a beautiful animal that people often take for a walk on a leash and might enter in some odd contest to try to win*

strange prizes. My dear, a better question for Hafiz would have been, 'How does it feel to be a heart?' For all I know is love, and I find my heart infinite and everywhere!'[65]

Zenith went on, "As we embark on the adventure to follow the dreams of our heart and the dreams of our infinite self, we must not only get comfortable with our feelings but we must be willing to let them lead us with an internal kind of strength and a more instinctive kind of knowledge. Then, just as I said earlier this evening, regardless of whether you identify as a man or a woman, 'You will open up to your vast potential (like a woman) and impregnate the world with a river of diamonds (like a man).'"

III
YOU

"Now, the person representing you in the dream was not representative of the whole of you but rather that part of you who was not represented by the intuitive female character in your dream. When it comes to manifesting our desires, we are all split in consciousness during the manifestation process. Part of us accepts everything, believes all, claims our desire and intuits the way to the realization of our wish. The other half of our self may, at worst, oppose our wish or completely deny the possibility of its future existence in our life. At best, this part of our self, like the character that was represented by you in the dream, is simply unaware or not as confident as our intuitive self and is shocked when the curtain is pulled back and finds itself on center stage living out the 'lie' that its twin, the higher intuitive self has been affirming as possible and true all along."

Hearing this, Skyler questioned Zenith with genuine confusion. "Are you faulting me for not believing in a 'lie' and how do you justify that?"

Zenith nodded in comprehension and said, "As William Blake says, 'The fool who persists in his folly will become wise,'[66] and new thought author Neville Goddard echoes this claim with the explanation, 'An assumption, though false, if persisted in will harden into fact!'[67] Even Shakespeare advises one to, 'Assume a virtue if you have it not,'[68] because he knows that if you play the part well enough, eventually that virtue will be woven into the very fabric of your being, which will clothe you in ever new circumstances as you perform upon greater stages of existence and merely watch as the walls of your world continue to expand."

Zenith continued, "Did the first doctor have an educational degree in healing? How could she when such degrees didn't even exist yet? Or did she just play the part of mastering her art until others recognized her as a master of the internal concept that she initially and boldly held of herself? Just as Geppetto persisted in his false wish to make his created toy into a real boy, even so you must persist with Pinocchio's nose and courage in the belly of the fish, until the fairy of the universe waves her wand, enchants your dreams and gives genuine life to your every wish. Your intuition knows that it can accomplish anything, but this can be a "lie" to that part of our self that is not yet concretely schooled in confidence. It can even be a lie to onlookers in your life who have not yet been sufficiently introduced to the internal power of the deepest self. Ultimately, the goal is that every part of us becomes more and more comfortable in discarding doubt and donning the fulfillment of our deepest desires."

"Even though this character, who didn't know himself nor his inherent worth, was played by you in your dream, you can now choose to live in greater harmony with your intuitive nature or with the higher 'chick' within you, as you said earlier." Skyler rolled his eyes and smirked at Zenith's quirkiness as if to say, *"You got me!"* and Zenith flashed her eyebrows at him, shrugged and shot him a triumphant grin. Then she continued, "You might be familiar with the George Bernard Shaw quote that says, 'The reasonable man adapts himself to the world: the unreasonable one persists in trying to adapt the world to himself. Therefore, all progress depends on the unreasonable man.'"[69]

"Or woman!" Skyler said, attempting to one-up her.

"Look at you, staying one step ahead of the game. I think you're really catching on now, aren't you, sweetheart!" Zenith said, with shocked facial expressions and humorous surprise in her tone. They both laughed and she continued, "There is a saying that says, 'There is no coal of character so dead that it will not glow and flame if but slightly turned.'[70] Your intuitive self is not dead, but until now she has been suffocating. Give her some space to thrive and she will help you pull greatness from the depths of your being."

IV
OVERCOMING THE FEAR YOUR SELF WORTH

"One of the greatest concepts in this dream was fear. Darling, your fear was so palpable that it was almost a character itself in that it completely hijacked and took over your other emotions of self worth, gratefulness and positive astonishment at what you had received. Although the fear that you experienced in this dream came in response to your concept of financial security, it was representative of the sum total of all fears that can keep you from attaining your higher consciousness or intuitive consciousness. If you succumb to it, as you have been in the repeated cycle of doing, my love, fear can keep you strapped into the consciousness of the old mentality or your old life even when you have already let go of your old life by resigning from your job."

"Now, if you are up for it, I want you to close your eyes and repeat after me," Zenith said.

"Ok," Skyler replied tentatively wondering where she was taking this.

Zenith continued, "I am always safe, I am always protected, I am always courageous and always fearless."

Skyler repeated after her slowly as if trying not to stumble over his words, "I am always safe, I am always protected, I am always courageous and always fearless."

"Again," Zenith said with the authority of a voice coach instructing a professional singer, "I am always safe, I am always protected, I am always courageous and always fearless."

Skyler repeated her words a little more firmly this time.

"Again!" Zenith said, whenever Skyler finished until he had said it seven or eight times and it was apparent that the phrase was becoming his own.

Then she said, "These are simple little phrases, but they hold inestimable power to redirect your mind away from the fear consciousness while establishing a magnetic and unstoppable force of boldness, valor and bravery."

"Wow!" Skyler said, "The effects of that saying were almost instantaneous for me. It felt really good. It's hard to explain but it was like there was an eraser that was wiping out every thought of anxiety in my mind with each utterance that I spoke as new feelings of confidence and well being were scribbled in their place. How is it that I've never known this nor used it before?"

Zenith shrugged and replied, "That's what good affirmations that resonate with us concerning any subject of life are supposed to do, my friend. It doesn't matter what the provoking issue of anxiety is, you can repeat this affirmation silently to yourself or out loud if you are alone whenever you feel fear beginning to rise up within you."

"Sounds good, yeah I think I will," Skyler said still marveling at the simplicity and effectiveness of the exercise.

"In your dream," Zenith went on, "since the check that you had received was a check that had no other name on it but your own, in all actuality, as the old saying goes, you had 'nothing to fear but fear itself.' In other words, fear was the only thing standing in the way of you making it to the bank. Taking your mind off of that fear, which was not real and had no substance, the fear itself would have to dissipate and vanish into thin air.

Remember, some situations are just like bad dreams, they're only unbearable while we're giving them our full attention. In this case, your wildest dream of attaining one of your deepest desires of financial abundance and security was suddenly turned into a nightmare by letting an unfounded fear fill your thoughts. The check, which was symbolic of all the security in the world for you could not produce any security in you if you had no security in yourself."

"On the flip side, if you took upon yourself the consciousness of your intuition played by the female character in your dream, you would have to embody the truth that she articulated in the dream. Since the man who died was you, in all actuality, the way to take on this consciousness is to repeatedly and feelingly affirming the state, 'I know that I am financially loaded and set for life.' The process of producing abundance and financial security begins within oneself by getting a new vision and letting it permeate and dominate one's thinking and feeling states through and through. Since what you perceive always perpetuates itself, you will soon find proof of your perception beginning to project itself in your world. As Neville Goddard says, 'The proof that you are will follow the consciousness that you are.'"[71]

Zenith went on, "And as Genevieve Davis teaches through her *Course in Magic* titles, you yourself must 'become magic'[72] before you can manifest it. You become magic, my dear, in either one of two ways. You can simply accept the fact that you are magic and that it is the natural state of your being. Or you can repetitively burn it into your being through coaching yourself in affirmations, meditations and visualizations until you have seared your ideal into the steel of your subconscious mind. Either way, when you do, you will discover through your own powers of wizardry within you that 'your word is your wand' by which you'll create a 'world of wonders' as Florence Scovel Shinn teaches."[73]

"By affirming new realities within yourself, you cultivate the psychological paradise of a new consciousness and as I love to say, 'You keep planting new seeds until your mind becomes the earth that gives birth to new worlds.' Of course, this new way of thinking would take a kind of dying to yourself in order to now embody the new you. But for you to know this at a deep level is to throw off the illusion of all fear and declare concerning living into the largeness of your desire that, 'Nothing's standing in my way like nothing's my security' in the words of the iconic hip hop artist, Lil Wayne.'"[74]

"You don't leave any stones unturned, do you?" Skyler teased.

"Why should I!" Zenith smirked and proudly asserted, "You can find genius anywhere and I intend to find it everywhere."

V
THE MAN AND HIS ASSOCIATE

"Finally, concerning the man and his associate that came to you in the dream, they represent both the asking and the fulfillment of desire. The man, who first entered, simply said that there was a man outside who had an envelope for you and asked if the man outside had your permission to come in. Everything outside of us is a potential desire seeking our attention. Through attention, we enter into the world of others and welcome them into our own. However, nothing can come into the world of our consciousness to stay until or unless we invite it, welcome it or give it our permission to stay. To give anything our attention is to pull it out of the darkness of space as an extra and give it a star role in the theatre of our existence."

"Manifestation expert Esther Hicks, teaches that we are constantly launching rockets of desire into the universe and the universe is always responding to our desires with an unequivocal and indestructible *yes* although we often shut the door on our own desires by inattention and focusing on contradictory feelings.[75] As soon as you ask, the universe starts to produce, package and set the route to deliver your request. When your inner desire aligns with the outer manifestation of your desire, it eventually shows up at your door and asks to come in."

"Just as these men came to you when you were wanting to know if you'd made the right decision to leave your job, time and time again, I have now shown up in your life because your desire to understand the contents of your dream was so strong that it was literally killing you. Intense burning desire is so magnetic, darling, that it will bring you anything that you ask for as you give it your persistent and focused attention. But, and this is a very big but," Zenith said humorously while smiling as she flashed her eyebrows at Skyler and made a smooth gesture of slapping her hip, "you must always remember that it was the passion in your asking and not your doomsday mentality that brought me to you, my love."

Zenith pressed on, "All of us have times of doubt and uncertainty and these can even be a kind of healthy release at times. However, continued focus on the negative can be as toxic as drinking battery acid rather than using the battery acid for what it was made for. Namely, it's made to charge the things in your life with surges of positive and useful energy. It is as Neville Goddard says, 'If we were to become as emotionally aroused over our ideals as we become over our dislikes, we would ascend to the plane of our ideal as easily as we now descend to the level of our hates.'[76] At this point, Skyler was once again reminded of his appointment with the bridge and his plans to descend from it.

He recognized that Zenith meant her words to do just that— remind him. He also knew that she obviously cared deeply for his wellbeing and he genuinely appreciated that she wasn't one to press the issue, expose his wound and rub it in. Just then, Zenith's encouraging nature reminded him of an Asian proverb that he'd recently stumbled upon while he was out to lunch with co-workers at a restaurant. The words had read, "The master is content to serve as an example and not to impose her will. She is pointed but doesn't pierce. Straight forward, but supple. Radiant but easy on the eyes."[77]

When Skyler had broken the fortune cookie open, for some reason it was like time slowed down as he focused, trying to decipher the meaning of these words and tuning out of the conversations that were taking place around his table. The words on the strip were so intriguing to him that he had pasted them into the web browser on his phone in order to explore them further. The words led him to Lao Tzu the ancient spiritual teacher who penned the words and who used similar simple sagely wisdom and paradoxical proverbs to help others experience the harmony of life. Skyler stumbled upon proverbs from the guru such as, "The path into the light seems dark,"[78] and "Mastering others is strength but mastering yourself is true power."[79] He was so enthralled by the writings that by the time one of his colleagues inadvertently snapped him out of his trance by throwing up his hand and signaling, "Waiter!", in order to call for the check, Skyler had already read half of *The Tao Te Ching*, which was the book where he found the quote that was inside of his fortune cookie.

That night as he drove home from the restaurant, Skyler's imagination got away from him and he thought about what it would be like if there were still characters like Lao Tzu who could help to guide others into the good life. Reminiscent of some of the characters in his books, he wondered what it would be like to have a mentor in the same way that Dante had Virgil, Telemachus had Athena and Boethius had Lady Philosophy. He wondered what it would be like to have his own Lao Tzu in the same way that Carlos Castaneda had Don Juan, C.S. Lewis had George MacDonald or even in the way that Khalil Gibran gave *The Prophet* to the islanders of Orphalese. What would it be like if he had his own guide like *Ishmael* or even Zarathustra?

Now, fully present back in the coffee shop, time stood still for Skyler once again, as he remembered that specific evening on which he had left the restaurant. The memory of Zarathustra, the sagely character from Nietzsche's book *Thus Spoke Zarathustra* who came down from his high place in the mountains to instruct the townspeople with his message of superior insight, struck Skyler like a hammer driving a peculiar and quite bizarre thought into his mind. It struck Skyler like a pendulum strikes the side of a bell, making the whole thing shiver and reverberate in the awakening of sound. Skyler's thoughts were loud as he pondered within himself inquisitively, "Zarathustra!" The thought came like eureka! A connection clicked in Skyler's consciousness and his memories from that evening in the restaurant aligned with his awareness of the present situation that he found himself in with Zenith.

What were the chances that this strange woman sitting before him who was quite magically and mystically mentoring him through following his dream just before he went to the bridge, reminded him of the ancient teacher Lao Tzu from his fortune cookie and Zarathustra who had just happened to be the first person that Zenith had quoted once they sat down for coffee. And now that he thought about it, earlier Zenith had even quoted Lao Tzu himself saying 'We join spokes together in a wheel, but it is the center hole that makes the wagon move. We shape clay into a pot, but it is the emptiness inside that holds whatever we want. We hammer wood for a house, but it is the inner space that makes it livable. We work with being, but non-being is what we use.'[80] For some reason, earlier that night, he'd had a hard time remembering why that quote felt so familiar to him, but now everything was crystal clear. He had breezed through that quote on the night that he was reading through *The Tao* in the restaurant. Skyler's head was a cave now and a songlike refrain of Zenith's words from earlier were echoing from deep within his brain saying, *"I'm not a fortune teller, I'm more of a fortune maker . . . fortune maker . . . fortune maker . . . fortune maker . . ."*

It couldn't be a coincidence that just weeks ago, Skyler had opened a fortune cookie in a restaurant that was so mysterious that it had him pondering, wondering and dreaming about having his own Lao Tzu or Zarathustra type character to guide him into the way of becoming all that he sought in his dream. And now, the world and his previous reality had actually bent in accordance to what he thought was a pretty insignificant and purely childish wish. It hit him like a ton of bricks. The yawning sun of a new day was somehow rising inside of him and stretching out its arms like tentacles across the expanses of his mind. When he looked up from being deep in thought, Zenith was still just sitting there sipping her water. No words were exchanged between them, but it felt like she had just slapped him with all of her might, then gripped him by his collar and said, *"Do you see it now? Do you see? You created and have brought all of this about! You set your intention and it appeared! You set your zenith, and here I am!"*

Although he still didn't *believe* it, something better and more grounded than belief had developed inside of him. Deep down Skyler *knew* that *he* had bent reality and summoned the guru who was sitting before him. Although she had given no examples, earlier Zenith had suggested that Skyler's own story could prove that the mind was magnetic. He had let his sea of questions go unanswered at the time, but now he knew that their relationship was exactly what she had been speaking of. There was no other explanation for what he was now experiencing, and because he finally knew at a cellular level that this whole scenario was his doing—that he had used his thoughts to create and manifest the magic of this reality, he ultimately felt something that he had certainly never felt before.

Searching for the feeling, it registered. He felt . . . he had felt *heard.*

Skyler didn't feel heard like a friend hears you when your world comes crashing down and it seems as if their ear and their companionship are the only solid ground for you to stand upon.

He had experienced that on innumerable occasions before especially with his wife, Tulip who could listen to him all day, name his feelings with precision and still ask the perfect questions that could draw a whole night of good conversation from the depths of his being.

As validating as that kind of being heard was to him, this was different. This felt like every cricket, every blade of grass, the sun, moon and stars and even all of existence had heard him. Not only did he feel that all of outer existence had heard him but that it had actually *answered back.* This was like every small, large and insignificant thing on the planet from the various wonders of the world such as Niagara Falls and the Yosemite Canyon right down to an inconsequential cricket's wings knew his innermost desires and had joined in to correspond with him, their conductor, in a resoundingly orchestrated symphony of sound.

Skyler felt that the universe was no longer asleep, but it was alive and animated in the same way that a puppet show gives life to lifeless, impossible and unassuming objects and animals that were deaf and mute only moments ago. In an instant, they know everything and humorously carry on conversation as if it were the most perfectly natural thing in the world. He now knew from personal and undeniable experience why some yogis from the East spoke of life as being "Lila" or a divine game. He felt as if lifelike constellations from another galaxy in space had heard his deepest musings from home base and after discussing it amongst themselves, they'd decided to pitch him a sign that was so bright that he couldn't miss it. They had indeed pitched him a grand slam floater that was so enlightening that he couldn't miss *her.*

Skyler didn't say anything to Zenith concerning everything that he was thinking and all that he had discovered. There was nothing to say that wasn't already written all over her face, which held a gentle comprehension, a soft compassion and the trace of a mild smile. Everything about her seemed to whisper, *"I know, my love. I know."* There was nothing left to add that Zenith hadn't already shared in depth with him all throughout the night. But, although Skyler was, even now in the silence between them, more captivated by Zenith than he had been all night, now there seemed to be something about her in the back of his mind that bothered him. After feeling perfectly connected with her for nearly the whole evening, there was something in her emotions now that he somehow couldn't read or even access. It was like an unbearable itch that he was mentally unable to scratch. He figured it would come to him or that she would simply address it when the time was right. And so once again he let it go, for the moment.

8 THE PAIN OF DEPARTING

After a few minutes of meaningful silence between them and fully recognizing that Skyler had absorbed the full weight of his memories, Zenith went on as if she was a seamstress who had already woven the robes and clothed the mystery of their evening together in perfect measure, before now coming to her completion by crowning the majesty of a magnificent night with one final conclusion. She began, "Every once in a while, you will have a dream or a vision that comes from the core of your being and the center of yourself, revealing what you've whispered to yourself today and how to live your deepest desires tomorrow."

"When these impulses come to you, consider yourself to be an intuitive expert by simply listening to yourself and following your good feelings for what you want. You don't have to know everything about everything in order for the universe to start working for you. You just have to know what makes you feel good and how to continue following that feeling until your world conforms to the vision that you carry. Become familiar with molding your inside world and then your outside world will magically reflect what you've established within it."

"Accept these dreams, visions or heightened experiences of awareness as positive messages from the universe, your infinite self or your higher intuitive self. If you never receive any dreams or messages, it doesn't matter. Simply create visions of what you want for yourself and flood your consciousness with them. In reality, as you now know, the universe is so animated that it is always speaking to you, conversing with you and sending you messages whether you are aware of this ongoing communication or not. But whether you create these messages yourself or receive them from your broader perspective, your consciousness is like a dam and can only hold so much before the reality of the vision that you hold within bursts forth into your outer world. The power of your vision does not lie in *how* your vision comes to you. It doesn't matter whether your vision is something that you've intentionally created within or whether it was a dream received from the universe."

"Again, the power doesn't lie in *how* your vision comes to you, the power lies in how *you* come to your vision. So, come to it with a repeated willingness to accept a new concept of your self and come to it with the thrill of believing into being what you've already seen within and know to be true. That is all that matters in relation to anything that you want in this life. Let these experiences, these visions and this awareness of what you desire dominate your thinking and give you new shoes to grow into, new dwellings to occupy, new art or new inventions to create and new aspirations to embody. Keep your dreams and your visions to yourself until you've fixed them so firmly in your mind that any possible doubts that can arise from others are as unnoticeable as a breeze that passes you by without a thought."

"Sweetheart!" Zenith said compassionately before she paused for a long moment peering deeply into Skyler's eyes. And in an incredible way it felt like Zenith's eyes were not only looking through him but crawling all over the core of his existence. "I have truly been running my mouth all night and I have loved our time together, but I really must be going now. Let me close with these words so that you too can get back to your affairs and your family, who will surely be worried sick about you. There is a quote by Ayn Rand that truly summarizes all that I have wanted to share with you tonight. She says, 'Do not allow your fire to go out, spark by irreplaceable spark in the hopeless swamps of the not-quite, the not-yet and the not at all. Do not let the hero in your soul perish in lonely frustration for the life you deserve and have never been able to reach. The world you desire can be won. It exists. It is real. It is possible. It is yours.'"[81]

Skyler could see it clearly now. It was indeed a new emotion within his friend that he couldn't scratch earlier. Zenith had held it back then, but the tears were speaking volumes now. He wasn't sure if they originated from the joy of the connection that they quickly established together or whether it was sadness that they must soon depart, some mixture of both or something entirely different. Either way, Skyler wanted to thank Zenith for a magical evening, he wanted to thank her for her energy and her care.

But he didn't know how to say it and the words refused to come. So, he simply got up and told her by doing what he wanted to do most. He opened his arms and she fell into them in a moment of firm and meaningful embrace for what seemed like hours fading into forever. Here every molecule of his being was buzzing with excitement, enlightenment and purpose in service to this woman who had somehow overseen the mass production of honey from the depths of his soul. The feeling of this embrace was infinitely more powerful than any words could express because

Skyler wasn't giving Zenith some stale and recycled platitude of gratitude. He was giving her his everything.

Here his heart exploded under the full weight of everything that happened that night and he knew that he could not still go to the bridge with the same intention that he had earlier even though some overpowering force of nature still compelled him to go there. But for what, Skyler didn't know. Being in Zenith's arms felt like a cosmic event in that he could feel how he was connected to everything, held by everything and holding everything. Without thinking about it, he shifted slightly, brushed one of her tears away with his thumb and said softly, "What's that saying that you said to me earlier, 'The harder a baby cries, the sweeter it dreams?'" Although Zenith playfully pounded on Skyler's chest with a solid whack from a closed fist and they both laughed initially, this broke the dam and Zenith cried out from a deep place now letting the tears flow unrestricted like the first rain of existence soaking her hair and his shirt through with the hurricane of her emotions.

At this point, something primal quaked and erupted in Skyler as well. It was like he realized that he couldn't beat her or laugh her tears away, so eventually he simply let go and joined her as all of his conflicting feelings from the past twenty years or so were given free expression. He too seemed to flood the room with his own tsunami of emotion caused by the tectonic shifting beneath the surface of his life. With their eyes closed and their heads buried in one another's shoulder they laughed. They broke. They wailed. And they bonded.

As if nature itself wanted to join in, a deafening thunderclap boomed outside as lightning ripped through the atmosphere illuminating the night. The sky opened and it too flooded the earth with its own timely and orchestrated cyclone of turbulent feelings. Although they both heard it and felt it, the newly discovered soul mates were too lost in the warmth of their embrace to open their eyes and take it all in. As far as they were concerned, they had come together as their own eye of the storm—a pinnacle of nature to be observed rather than being the observers.

For that miniscule moment in time, they were the storm itself to be chased rather than being its chasers. In that moment, absolutely nothing could disrupt them nor penetrate their presence. After a few millennia however, the pain began with what felt like the feeling of a massive hangover and suddenly Skyler realized not only that Zenith had made him feel more spectacular than he'd ever felt before, but that his departure from her was going to be much more excruciating than he ever could have expected.

THE PILGRIMAGE TO THE BRIDGE

Since only one person in every fifty survives a fall into water from a height of two hundred feet or greater, the college students who saw the man hurdling down towards the water like a wrecking ball, were all certain that he was dead. The students had been camping out in the woods alongside the river that flows beneath Everest Bridge when they heard the angry shouts from up on the bridge. Then came the terrifying screams from onlookers as the man plummeted to his doom.

Reports later stated that a woman with her twin babies in the car had pulled to the side of the bridge and three late-night joggers had also stopped when they noticed a belligerently intoxicated man who appeared to be in a fierce argument with his shadows. Before they even had a chance to speak to the man and capture his attention, the man awkwardly scrambled up onto the rail without warning and pushed himself backwards off of it. One account said that the man appeared to be so angry that he pushed the rail itself like it was a person and seemed to be still arguing with his shadows "or whoever" for the few seconds that it took for him to hit his target below.

Though it was dark, through the well-illumined bridge and the city lights, the college students who'd been at their bonfire in the woods below, never lost sight of Skyler once he hit the water. Two of them, one girl and one guy were experts in the water and courageously managed to swim the length of two football fields in what felt like near freezing temperatures in order to grab hold of Skyler's body before it was swept out to sea. Those students who had remained behind and many of the drivers who had then begun to pile up on the bridge had already called for help. The rescue crew had managed to arrive, and they were there to assist the swimmers by running into the water when the students that were dragging the lifeless body in from the deep were still thirty yards from the shore.

The bones in his feet, ankles and shins had turned to soup upon contact with the deep water that had solidified into a sea of concrete at the vehicular speed at which Skyler was traveling when he fell. Although the injuries all throughout his body were extensive and recovery would be months long, his feet and legs, taking the major portion of the impact, had prevented fatality by somewhat shielding many of his vital organs. His wife, Tulip, and his teenage kids' emotional stability had almost been more shattered than Skyler's physical body. They knew that Skyler had been disappointed by his work situation, but they never imagined that he would ever do anything like this. After all of the major operations had been completed, the doctor told Skyler's family that although his life would be completely different than it was before, he would most likely recover after months of procedures and therapy. Although still crushed, this news gave Skyler's family a renewed optimism and they visited him every day while desperately waiting for him to wake up.

After weeks passed however, and the medical team took the breathing tube out of Skyler's throat with no immediate response, it was only his wife, Tulip, who came everyday while his kids completed their studies and extra curricular activities during the week then returned again on the weekends. One day while Tulip was reading at his bedside, Skyler smiled, rolled onto his side and wrapped his arms around the thin air as if he was holding someone. Before long, a tear trickled down his face. Then another came and another raced until he was bawling uncontrollably. Tulip yelled for help and though Skyler was all right, it took twenty minutes before the nurses and assistants were able to pry his arms open and get them to relax from being in the position of embrace.

10 AWAKEN- ING

After calming him down and letting him sleep for another few hours, Skyler finally awoke asking his wife about the woman who saved him from the bridge.

Tulip responded gracefully, "Honey, it wasn't a woman who saved you, it was a group of college kids."

"But the lady at the shops!" Skyler corrected.

"You're not at the shops, hun, you're in the hospital . . . It's ok, honey, you're confused!" Tulip comforted, "The doctors said all of this would be normal and expected."

Unsatisfied, Skyler went on, "Why am I at the hospital? Listen, hun! I went to the bar intending to have a few drinks . . ."

Tulip briskly cut in, "A few drinks is right! You were incredibly thirsty! The bartender said that you had ordered forty shots! He thought you were ordering for a whole group, but it was just you there and no one else arrived, Skyler. After fifteen or so you passed out. I don't know whether to be thankful that you never made it closer to forty or not considering the circumstances. Maybe drinking more would have kept you safely at the bar so that you could get some serious help before the alcohol killed you. Anyway, when you woke up you swiftly took several more shots before you paid your tab and left. With that much alcohol in your system, I don't even know how you . . ." she trailed off in exasperation.

"I know, Tulie! It was a crazy night . . . But after I left, I met this woman at the shops before I ever made it to the bridge. We stayed there and talked for hours! She talked me out of it so that I never went to the bridge! It was amazing, hun! She was like some fortune teller or something. She knew I was heading to the bridge and that I was going to do something stupid! She knew about my dreams and she explained everything and made it all crystal clear, hun!" Tulip just sat there and looked at him with a blank expression. Skyler wasn't upset but he was getting frustrated that she just wouldn't say whatever it was that she was feeling. At the same time, he couldn't help but fondly being reminded of how well her name fit her because as he often told her, *"You're like a tulip that's still gorgeous even when you just can't open up."*

However, focusing on the matter at hand, Skyler began to pry, "What? What does that look mean, hun? Why are you looking at me like that?" Skyler begged, "Oh I get it. You don't believe me, do you?"

Tulip hesitated before speaking her mind, "Babe, it's not that I don't believe you. It's just that . . . what you're saying just doesn't add up, Sky!" she groaned. "The bartender said that you left the bar at 11:00 P.M. But the joggers that saw you at the bridge said that they saw you arguing with your shadows at the bridge before they saw you jump without warning at 11:17 P.M. That means you had to have left the bar and gone straight to the bridge. I don't even know how you made it there at all in your condition. But don't you see, babe? There was no time for you to stop and talk to anyone or even have an hour-long conversation, much less one that lasted for hours as you say."

Skyler was stupefied and completely dumbfounded as he pondered what Tulip was saying. But somehow it was beginning to make sense as a different narrative developed and coalesced in his mind. He never stopped at the shops on the way to the bridge, so he couldn't have possibly met Zenith there. But he had met her. That much he was sure of. He argued with his shadows at the bridge, then turned and thought that he would see his reflection in the window but there was no window there because there were obviously no windows at the bridge. There was only the water. Zenith had met him in the water and now he knew that he had indeed . . . jumped. He had jumped! . . . and somehow, he was still . . . alive?

Yes, he must have met Zenith upon impact. This is why she was sad, he remembered. *"Zenith knew . . . what I was going to have to endure in order to recover,"* Skyler thought to himself. After piecing a vague, yet somewhat satisfactory picture of this whirlwind of scattered puzzle pieces together in his mind, Skyler became somber and dejected before regretfully asking, "So what's the damage, hun?"

Tulip looked at Skyler for some time questioning herself and observing him as if to say, *"You sure you're ready to open that door?"* But something shifted within her as she came to a quick conclusion and she cautiously warned, "Brace yourself, Sky . . . As you can imagine . . . it ain't pretty."

As Tulip slowly turned down the blankets, Skyler noticed with utter astonishment that both of his legs were completely gone from the knee down. In addition, his forearms had been casted down to his hands in hopes of temporarily stabilizing the plates, pins and screws that had been surgically placed in his wrists. Skyler stared in horror at his new body and at what he had done. How could he do this to himself and his family? How had he survived? What would his new life consist of? As he sat there speechless, taking it all in, Tulip fell to her knees at his bedside, untied his right wrist restraint from the bed, laid her head in his lap and wept and wept and wept as Skyler awkwardly stroked her hair with a casted wrist.

Although Skyler sat there in shock, as he took it all in, this scene reminded him of how he and Zenith had cried together. It was a cry that he had needed but he just hadn't known how to do in years. He also remembered that Zenith had explained that, *"If we learn to cross them properly, the rivers that we cry can lead us to oceans of invincible happiness. As the mystical poet Rumi likes to say, 'Where there is ruin, there is great treasure' and as I like to say, 'You see yourself as a shipwreck, but we see your treasure glowing inside, beneath the oceans in your eyes.'"* He heard Zenith saying as he also remembered swimming through the wreckage and finding the massive vault of rubies, diamonds, gold and silver.

Everything that they'd talked about came rushing back in now. He remembered how he had felt alive, understood, connected and energized with Zenith. He remembered how Zenith had come in response to his childish wish that night after he had left the restaurant and how this realization had helped him to know forever that the universe could hear his deepest longings and was in full communication with him. He also remembered feeling confident, like there was nothing he couldn't do when he was with Zenith. She made him feel like he could conquer the world. And finally, he remembered how both of them had laughed when he quoted her words saying, *"The harder a baby cries, the sweeter it dreams."* The memory brought a genuine smile all the way from the center of himself as it bubbled up to the surface of Skyler's face. Although he kept silent about all of this, he now knew at a gut level what it meant to experience the invincible happiness that Zenith had told him about as Tulip lay there bawling in his lap and he too let the tears come streaming down his face.

REHAB AND THE CODE BLUE

Months went by and Skyler never spoke of the woman who saved him from the bridge again. However, he used everything that Zenith had taught him in order to build a new mindset, aid him in his recovery and bring all kinds of things to him that his family needed but couldn't afford in their previous circumstances much less their new state of affairs. He acquired such things as paid camps and counseling for his kids, which were all much needed after everything they'd been through. After speaking with the nursing manager of his floor, the manager was able to pull some strings, which led to a new part time job at the hospital for Tulip who'd been let go of her previous position because of how much work she'd missed while focusing on Skyler's recovery.

And Skyler even managed to score a pair of the most high-tech, low-weight and most comfortable prosthetic legs on the market. Even with all of this, Tulip continued to worry. She worried about the future, she worried about the past and she worried about the kids' ability to cope. Now that Skyler was safe and she couldn't worry about his physical health, she quite naturally shifted to worrying about his continued mental health and about the enormous medical bills that they would never be able to repay.

Skyler heard all of her concerns and he humbly owned and faced his responsibility for putting his family in the situation that they were now in, which was incomparably worse than the humble life that they'd previously managed to endure. To be honest, Skyler genuinely had no idea how they would ever be able to pay off the mountain of medical bills that they now faced. But he was so thrilled to be alive that it was hard for him to focus on any of those things for very long. He thought about how lucky he was to have a second chance and to have *most* of his faculties in tact.

Because of this, every part of him was radiant and vibrant with possibility. Zenith had told him that he could weed his mind and cultivate it into a psychological paradise and Skyler felt that he was actually doing that now. Although he didn't know how it would come, he knew what he wanted and he affirmed the reality of his dream over and over again. In the meantime, he read more and more of the writers that Zenith had told him about and he grew more and more contented with the treasures that he had in his present situation. He had his life, he had his mind, he had his health and he had his family.

One weekend, while he was undergoing physical therapy exercises in the hospital hall near the front lobby, a code blue was called over the hospital intercom signaling a respiratory emergency and a crowd of medical team officials came through the lobby rushing furiously with a patient on a medical bed in route to the operating room. A toddler who had been playing with his ball, lost control of it, ran after it and finally leaned down just in front of the rolling bed that was unable to stop. Seeing the disaster forming as if in slow motion, Skyler broke free from the safety grip of his physical therapist and leaped to push the toddler onto one of the lobby couches just before the boy would've been hit by the locomotive medical team.

Skyler fell down on all fours almost slamming his head into a glass award case and instantly heard the crack of one of his prosthetic legs as the bed rolled over it. Tulip had also just shown up to the hospital to check in on him and to bring Skyler some of his favorite hot chili topped with Mexican Cheese in a fresh sourdough bowl. Entering the lobby just as the code blue was called, Tulip watched with pride, fear and disbelief as she saw the child, she saw Skyler go down just after helping the boy to avoid certain disaster and she heard the loud snap of his high-tech new leg. Hanging his head to look at it, Skyler assessed the damage, but he already knew that it would need to be replaced.

Then, swiftly looking up to see how close he'd come to smashing his head into the award case, for a brief moment he locked eyes with Zenith's smiling reflection in the case instead of his own. She had been holding one award plaque in each hand. The award in her right hand had the distinct clavicle of a winged creature on it and the award in her left hand depicted the vertebrae of a human spine. Though Skyler was not able to make out the inscriptions on each award, he didn't need to. He remembered what Zenith had said about dreams taking time to build character and the meaning of her appearance at that precise moment was immediately obvious to him. It was as if Zenith was saying, *"Congratulations, Skyler . . . Your desire represented by this wishbone and the strength of your character represented by this backbone are now in alignment with one another."* Just like that however, Zenith's reflection vanished, and Skyler was faced to face with himself again.

Out of the corner of his eye, he also noticed his wife's reflection standing behind him with those gorgeous and adoring eyes filled with a mixed look of utter shock and deep concern. Looking into the glass, something deep within caused Skyler to say aloud, "I love you!" Of course, no one except Skyler had seen the guru in the glass and so those who observed the event thought that the hero with the prosthetic legs was just speaking to his wife who, after recovering her ability to move, immediately came to help him and the child back up again before delivering the boy safely to his parents.

The onlookers had no idea that there were layers and levels to that expression of Skyler's love. There were layers to his love in the same way that a song can have so many meanings to so many different listeners. There were layers to Skyler's love in the same way that a song can even take on different meanings to the same listener either in one instant or at various periods in that listener's life. Indeed, Skyler had been speaking to Tulip who'd loved him wholeheartedly in spite of everything that he had put her through and whose love for him had not faltered even once through the worst storm of his life. But Skyler had also been speaking to Zenith who he'd come to understand was a manifestation of his deepest and infinite self. In this sense, Zenith was similar to the man who'd died and left Skyler the $40 million check in his dream. In this sense, Zenith was also like the woman in the dream who had received a twin portion of the old man's wealth. Finally, at a very basic level, Skyler had been speaking to the reflection of his own image, whose reflection had also captured his attention after the guru had disappeared.

Skyler's image had been somewhat disfigured and mangled by his fall from the bridge. But even after undergoing these detrimental changes, Skyler no longer envied Narcissus, the mythical man known for loving his own image. Maybe this was partially what the guru had meant when she'd said that, *"Dreams are a lot like people, matter and energy. They can evolve from a less solid state to a more solid state and back again, but they can never be destroyed. Similarly, you can crush a mirror by dropping a wrecking ball on it, but its images and reflections will live on."* Even though Skyler's legs had evolved into a less solid state, he was still ecstatic to know that the rest of his reflection would simply live on in its current unharmed and healthy physical state instead of dissolving into dust after settling at the bottom of the sea.

Skyler now understood that you didn't have to be a mythical creature or even an egotistical one in order to love yourself, to love your reflection and ultimately to love your life. You simply had to have encounters with yourself and others that helped to introduce you to your true self, the real you. Zenith had been like a mirror for Skyler not only because he had first found her reflection in the window of the storefront as a substitute for his own, but ultimately because she had introduced him to the reflection of his true nature and had given him a new vision of himself.

It's been said that, "Talent hits a target that no one else can hit, while genius hits a target that no one else can see."[82] Likewise a great mentor, friend or mirror can tell you things about yourself that no one else will tell you, but an expert mirror will show you things about yourself that no one else can even see. Zenith had peered into the depths of Skyler's soul and had seen a splendid and brilliant creature that even surpassed Skyler's most generous secret and subconscious valuations of himself. Skyler had recently read a quote by the mystical poet Hafiz that had said, "One day, the sun admitted, 'I am just a shadow . . . I wish I could show you when you are lonely or in darkness the astonishing light of your own being.'"[83] In Skyler's view, this is exactly what Zenith had done for him when he was broken and washed up. She had shown him the undeniable radiance of his existence.

It was as if Zenith had pulled the sun from out of the sky, held it up before his eyes and said, *"This is your destiny, this is the way I see you. Notice how the sun never has an inferiority complex, it shines the same whether above or below. Notice how hating yourself is like hating the sun, no matter how much you complain of it agitating your eyes, its brilliance shines on. So darling, I keep holding up the mirror of the sun so you can see the stunning reflections of everything you're becoming."* Because of his encounter with Zenith, Skyler had come to realize for himself that most of the time we don't need new images, we just need new mirrors.

THE QUEST TO CREATE

I
UNEXPECTED VISITORS

That night, after Tulip had left, the nurse came in and told Skyler that some unexpected visitors were there to see him. Skyler told the nurse to tell the visitors that they could come on in. However, in his haste to get his legs back on before they arrived at his room, Skyler didn't secure his left leg properly. As a result, his first step towards the door faltered and he came tumbling down in a heap just as the first few of his eleven guests had entered the threshold of his hospital room. Although initially paralyzed with inaction at the gravity and recognition of what was happening, a young lady named Amber Blaze with her hair up in a tight bun almost immediately moved towards him and swooped down to assist the double amputee.

She then placed Skyler's arm over her shoulder and took a good close look at him while Skyler stared down trying to figure out what went wrong before another gentleman who was with Amber was able to lend his shoulder for Skyler's other arm. Skyler thanked them profusely as they helped him to get comfortably situated in his bed. As he got situated, he made a lighthearted comment to the group knowing that his reference was way before this youthful audience's time.

"You'll have to forgive me," Skyler said, "I want to roll like an old school Firebird when I grow up, but I'm still learning how to fly with my new set of wheels!"

They all laughed a little and waved away his apologies saying that this kind of thing was expected and that helping him back up was really no problem at all. As his company found chairs and began to settle in around the room, Skyler realized that he didn't immediately recognize any of them. He initially figured that they must be some of his kids' high school friends, but that he just wasn't able to place them yet for some unexplainable reason. So curiously, Skyler asked the youngsters, "Do I know you?"

They explained that although he did not know them, they knew him because they had been the college students who had called for help, swam to rescue him and pulled him back to the safety of the shore after he had fallen from the bridge. They further explained that they wanted to come to visit earlier but that they just couldn't find a time when all eleven of them could visit him together.

Skyler was so excited to finally meet and wholeheartedly thank these incredible young adults to whom he'd owed his life. On any other day and with any other people, he would have probably been more reserved. However, these youngsters were not any other people. They were not interested in surface introductions to a man that they felt genuinely tied to by some mysterious fate.

They wanted details and their questions came in rapid succession. They wanted to know what it felt like to fall from such a height, if he'd been afraid and what his major regrets were. They wanted to know if the newspapers and media had gotten his story right or whether he'd felt misrepresented. They wanted to know about his old legs and his new legs. In short, they wanted to know everything. But in the end, they wanted to know what made his life so bad that he'd actually go through with a suicide attempt from Everest Bridge. They wanted to know why he did it, what it was like to be in a coma for so long, what it felt like to be one of only two in a hundred people that had survived such a fall and if he ever wished that he wouldn't have survived at all. Not only were these youngsters fearless and shameless with their questions, this day was also special because it was the first time of many that Skyler had the opportunity to see Zenith again.

These two things made the meeting with the students much more magical than it might have been had the day's circumstances been different. Skyler completely opened up and shared everything. No question was off limits. He told them about Zenith, whom he was almost certain that he'd met upon impact with the water. He told them about how she knew about his dreams and explained the meaning of them, which had given him an entirely new outlook and perspective on life.

Skyler told them about how he'd already used what Zenith had taught him and everything that he'd recently been reading to acquire things that he should have never had access to in his financial situation. He also told them that he was fully confident that he would further use what she'd taught him in order to repay the mountainous medical bills that he now owed but which were in no way covered by his insurance. He even told them how he had been so excited to see Zenith again earlier that day. But ultimately, after three hours of answering their questions and sharing his heart with them, he told them that he had found the invincible happiness that came with the confidence of crossing the river of his tears on his quest to create a new life.

He concluded, "I guess what I've learned from all of this is that . . ." he paused briefly slightly choked up with the words, "sometimes we must gravitate towards madness before we can levitate on greatness."

The kids were deeply moved and impacted by the story of the man who'd lived to tell of how he'd fell from Suicide Bridge. Although they had varying opinions on what to think about every detail of the story, they thought the story, as a whole, was "bonkers", "intense" and "badass". The students weren't sure about whether the story was completely true or not and they didn't really care. For the moment, they were simply and genuinely happy for Skyler because he seemed to be so content with himself and radiant with new purpose, which was certainly much better than the condition that they had originally found him in. They were also amazed that they had been there on the shore that night to help him out of the water and that they had decided to return months later to meet him. Finally, they were astonished that their lives were forever entangled with the life of this mysterious myth of a man who had survived Everest.

Three of the students were leaders in the university's Student Government Association, and when they heard that Skyler was going to be discharged from the hospital that coming weekend, they thought it would be a daring yet noble idea to have Skyler visit their school to speak at a conference that was being held the following week, if he was up for it. One of the guest speakers had dropped out at the last minute and they had been desperately seeking someone to fill the open slot, without any success. In the end, if they were unable to find someone, the school would ultimately fill that spot with entertainment or a recess, but that was a worst-case scenario.

"How many students are we talking about here?" Skyler asked anxiously, since he had never actually spoken publicly to more than a handful of coworkers in his office.

"Oh just a few classes should be there. No more than seventy-five to a hundred students and a few faculty members," Amber lied. "Right guys?" she flashed her eyebrows at the two other students that were in the SGA hoping they'd follow her lead and play along for the good of the team.

When Skyler saw the raised eyebrows and rapid synchronized nods of the students' head movements agreeing in unison, he thought within himself. He'd always wanted to teach, and this was a small-scale chance for him to discover if he actually enjoyed the work or at least a portion of it. Even though he had never spoken to so many people at once before, he figured that one time couldn't be so bad. Could it? It wasn't like he was being asked to teach for the whole semester, and there was really no curriculum, but to simply tell his story. The opportunity made Skyler nervous, but he definitely wanted to share his story again. Just getting the chance to speak to the students that night charged him with an energy that was strangely reminiscent of being with Zenith herself.

When Amber saw him mulling her question over within himself, she begged, "Come on Mr. Skyler! Suicide is a serious issue that our students struggle with directly or indirectly, and I know your story could help so many other people who are going through what you have been through."

That was all that Skyler needed to hear. He had become so focused on his anxiety around speaking that he had forgotten about his dream of getting his story out so that he could help others who were struggling just like he had been. He admitted to himself that getting his story out through writing an autobiography or even screen writing was a much more appealing option to him than speaking publicly, but something told him that this was a great place to begin to organize his thoughts about what he wanted to convey.

He also felt that he owed his life to these kids and although it might be challenging, this was a small price to pay for everything that they'd done for him.

"Ok," Skyler said. "I'll do it! My only request is that you all drop the 'Mr. Skyler'. I hate formalities. It's just Skyler. Is that cool?" Skyler said with a firmness that wouldn't let him disguise his underlying annoyance.

"No problem Skyler," and "Sure thing, Sky," some of the students agreed while taking the opportunity to abbreviate his name even further."

With that, one of the students said in a parting tone, "Thanks so much for speaking with us tonight." A chorus of "Yeah, thanks Skyler!" followed this, as a whole host of other expressions of thanks rang out from around the room.

"No problem," Skyler said before continuing, "And honestly, I wouldn't be here if it weren't for all of you. So really, thank you! I owe you my life!" As tired as Skyler was, he wasn't going to miss this opportunity to get up out of his bed and look every one of those students in the eyes in order to genuinely connect with and individually thank each one of them before they went on their way. So, one by one, eight of the students came up, introduced themselves further, conversed a bit, added a few parting words, shook Skyler's hand and gave him a hug, or some mixture thereof.

Meanwhile Bryan and Micah, the two other Student Government leaders that had kept quiet earlier, shot daggers at Amber before dragging her outside of Skyler's room and far enough down the hall so that they were out of earshot.

"Seventy-five to a hundred students and a handful of professors, Amber? What the hell was that about? There's going be well over ten thousand people at that event!" Bryan viciously interrogated.

Amber responded nonchalantly, "Skyler will do just fine. Did you hear him tonight, he loves talking about this stuff, and he's seriously a natural? Anyway, it really isn't even about him, it's about all those people who are going to benefit from hearing his story. If this talk saves one person from living through the hell that Skyler has had to live through, wouldn't it all be worth it?" Amber questioned in an unconcerned tone hoping to deescalate their anger.

"Well of course it would be worth it, but that's assuming that Skyler will even be able to deliver once he sees the size of the crowd! I still think we should've just told him the truth!" Bryan said before Micah cut into the conversation. "Yeah! What if he has a nervous breakdown or something? You never know what effects stress can have on someone before they're put in an unexpected situation. And it's not like Skyler doesn't already have a history of succumbing to stress."

At this point, Amber waved away their concerns with her hand, "You all are overreacting and completely blowing this thing out of proportion. Did you hear him tonight? There's an unshakeable depth in that man and I know there's so much more that we haven't even discovered yet."

Bryan fired back, "Just because someone with a troubled past says they have an invincible happiness now, doesn't mean that they don't have any triggers that can send them spiraling again at a moment's notice. You of all people should know that, Amber!" Bryan said this because depression had loomed large in Amber's family for generations and she had struggled with a few serious bouts of it despite her ability to keep a public appearance of holding herself together.

"I understand what you're saying, but this is different. After a suicide attempt, Skyler has been here in this hospital without legs for almost seven months living through what would be a nightmare to most people and he's not even phased by it. He's handling it like a champ. Trust me, he'll be fine. Of course, he'll get a little nervous, but just let me deal with that."

Amber's words held such an heir of confidence that Bryan instantly knew that she was hiding something, and it pressed him to dig deeper saying sharply, "What do you mean, Amber?" But the look on Bryan's face and the undertones of his voice implied, "And you better tell us everything!" "Look!" Amber said. "Remember when Skyler said that he fell in front of the bus on the way to the bridge?"

"Yeah! What of it?"

"And that there was a man there that tried to pull him up out of the puddle?"

"Yeah!" they said in unison.

"Well, that man was my business mentor Bruce Sikes."

"You mean the GQ billionaire investor that you meet with every week?" Micah asked.

"He's not a billionaire. He's a successful local entrepreneur and philanthropist who's serious about developing business minded students regardless of their major."

"Not gonna negate the GQ part, Amber?" Micah said sarcastically taunting Amber with a raised eyebrow and a knowing grin.

"Well listen, I'd be lying if I tried to deny that he's attractive . . ." Amber replied.

Just then, Bryan sternly cut in and redirected the conversation. "The reports didn't say anything about Bruce in connection with Skyler's suicide attempt. How could you possibly . . ." At this point, Micah quickly cut in again branching out on a limb as clarity formulated and the equation added up in his mind, "She knows that it was Bruce who helped Skyler out of the puddle . . . because she was the other person who also tried to help Skyler." Amber nodded silently in consent as the others looked at her in astonishment and disbelief.

Amber began quietly so that she'd be unable to be overheard. "I remember that night so vividly because I had just finished meeting for coffee with Bruce—as we do every week at Buzz Worthy—when we came out and saw the man on the rollerblades being pulled by the dogs which triggered the whole event. Even though, Bruce was headed to an important meeting and I was headed to class, everyone was just standing there, and we just knew that we had to do something to help . . . to let this broken man know . . . that we cared."

She had their full attention in her grip now and she kept on speaking, "Even though he pushed us both away and wouldn't have anything to do with us, we weren't mad. Well, maybe a little at first, but I know from experience what true depression is and I could tell by the look in his eyes that this man . . . Skyler . . . was truly depressed, crushed and defeated. However, at the time there was no way that either of us could have possibly known the traumatic events he was about to undergo at the bridge. Anyway, we weren't mad, and we didn't care that there was no time to change clothes and that both of us were going to have to make it to our separate destinations with shoes that were soaked through."

"Later we both joked . . ." Amber smirked pitifully, with tears streaming down her face before she went on. "Later we both joked that both of us would do it all over again just to let this poor man know that he mattered to us and that we cared. The crazy thing is that even after he fell from the bridge and Trenton and Ashley swam out to sea to bring him back . . . even after I watched them put him in the ambulance and I later read about his story in the newspaper, I still had no idea that it was the same person that Bruce and I had tried to help up out of the puddle that evening just outside of Buzz Worthy's."

"It wasn't until we all got to the hospital tonight and I saw him fall as he came to greet us at the door that . . . that I realized in a flash of understanding who he was and that . . . I was more tied to his story than any of us had previously known. The timing was too awkward to tell him right then and for a while I sat there stunned not truly believing it myself, while trying to piece it all together within me. But as I sat and listened to him speak and I saw how well he dealt with all of our prying and crazy questions, somehow it all began to sink in that this was the same man . . . and somehow, as crazy and contradictory as it sounds, I knew that this Skyler, who we met tonight, was not the same man that I helped up out of that puddle. There was no way that *that* man who was so beaten and destroyed, the man who had went to the bridge, could be the man who sat here and conversed with us tonight. The man we helped up out of that puddle was not, and could not be the same man who I helped up into the bed this evening."

Call it a hunch, intuition, personal experience or whatever, but just as I could tell by one look that the man coming up out of that puddle was deeply shattered within, I can see right now in the depths of his eyes and I can hear in his story, that Skyler has experienced something that many people who have serious depression and other forms of serious mental illness could only wish in their wildest dreams to encounter. Having lived through depression and anxiety myself since I was a kid, by pushing it down, getting counseling, fighting with it and just dealing with it the best I possibly can, I am familiar with it enough to recognize genuine healing when I see it. And I'm telling you guys that I see genuine healing in Skyler."

"Hearing his story here tonight, I thought to myself that our students have to hear this man speak and I vowed that I would do whatever it took to get him to speak at our event. I understand that you all might be disappointed and even upset with me for lying, but just as I would step down into that puddle again for him or anyone else in his position, I know that the open spot on our stage was made for Skyler and I would do anything to have him tell his story there! But even more than this being a great opportunity for our students, which it is, as a disabled man who has battled with mental illness, this could also be a great time of redemption and a re-entry point back into society for Skyler himself."

Bryan and Micah simply stood there, speechless, taking in Amber's words and her emotion. She continued, "When Bruce hears about this, he's going to flip. For months he has been secretly planning to donate a million dollars each, to three speakers' causes which they will be presenting at the conference. Imagine his surprise when he finds out that his donation may go to a man with a mountainous medical bill that he tried to help up out of a puddle on the street seven months ago. I am already setting up a Trigger Funding social media campaign that I will announce to the arena at the end of Skyler's speech. Even if Bruce decides not to help, and that is a very small chance knowing Bruce, if every person there just gives a few dollars we could put a good dent in Skyler's medical bill."

"I promise that my intentions are good, guys! Maybe I couldn't help him up out of that puddle seven months ago. But I'll be damned if I don't do everything in my power to help him get back on his feet again after what he has done for me here tonight. Well, metaphorically speaking," Amber shrugged, alluding to Skyler's amputations while hoping Bryan and Micah understood the heart of her vision. After a few moments, Amber broke the silence, "Listen, you all are gonna do what you're gonna do, but I have a nagging suspicion that Skyler is not only going to help a lot of people with his story, but that he can actually still really help me too. So . . . I'm going back in there to ask him a few more questions and get even more clarity before I hopefully get to fill him in on the details of the event." With that, Amber looked back and forth between Bryan and Micah, shrugged in surrender to whatever decision they made and went back in the room just as the other eight students were leaving. As she passed by, giving them all hugs, Amber said, "We'll catch up with you all soon. We just have a few loose ends we need to tie up for the conference."

"Sounds good," the group of eight responded as they parted for the evening.

Coming back into the room, Amber made some small talk around the date, time and purpose of the conference before coming to her deeper motive. "Skyler, if you have a few extra minutes, I was wondering if you could elaborate just a bit on something that you said earlier?"

"Which part?" Skyler asked.

Once Amber clarified her personal interest in relation to her own depression, Skyler addressed her question with more depth. He was then asked two follow-up questions about Zenith's concept of self worth and her concept of radiating a new reality by both Bryan and Micah who both chose to stay behind with Amber. When all was said and done, it was well beyond midnight before the last three students left and Skyler was finally able to get some much-needed rest.

II
BUSINESS DEALS AND BELLY FLOPS

One of the eight students named Jin, who had left earlier with the previous eight students, and who'd also sat to the side and appeared to Skyler to be disengaged and more interested in fumbling with his phone all throughout the conversation, happened to be a film major that was secretly recording the discussion. After departing from the others and editing it as best he could, with what he knew to be poor quality footage, he hit save and crashed for the night.

The next morning, he took the footage to his film instructor, Professor Donovan and said, "Are we filming any of the smaller satellite venues at the Spring Conference next week?"

Professor Donovan responded briefly peering up at Jin before returning his attention to his work, "Jin, I'm letting you film a handful of our star speakers for the conference this year and you're still looking to get more? What's up? I thought five speakers would be enough even for your ambitious appetite?"

"Well, the SGA is about to bring on a new speaker that would really be a personal project for me."

"Is that right?" Professor Donovan said without looking away from his computer screen. "Who is it?" Professor Donovan inquired nonchalantly.

"A man by the name of Mr. Skyler Deavensby."

"Wait a minute. Deavensby . . ." he said perusing his memory bank inquisitively. "You talking about that washed up old chap that cannon balled from Everest Bridge that you all pulled out of the river and who got plastered all over local news last fall? What are they trying to do, turn the Spring Conference into a charity campaign or something?"

"Beats me," Jin said before continuing, "But I think that he's going to be speaking at one of the smaller venues for our Spring Conference."

Utterly astounded as if he'd been previously in a fog awakening from a deep sleep before now and suddenly understanding the full meaning and significance of what Jin was saying, Professor Donovan replied, "First of all, how's that even possible? Deavensby's out of the coma and up on his feet again?"

"Well I wouldn't say that exactly," Jin answered "He's a double amputee, Doc. But he's alive, out of the coma and his mind is pretty sharp considering the circumstances."

"I'd have to see it to believe it, but I'll take your word for it and humor you for now. Second of all, Jin, there's another impossibility in your story."

"What's that?" Jin asked.

Professor Donovan responded, "There are no smaller venues at the Spring Conference. Every speaker that will speak there speaks at the main event."

"Are you sure? That's not what SGA leader, Amber Blaze is advertising."

"Am I sure? Amber Blaze can say whatever she likes, but I've been filming that event since long before both of you were born, my friend."

"Well, makes no difference to me," Jin said before continuing, "But we all went to see him the other day and I just thought you might want to hear a previously untold perspective from a local news sensation suicide survivor who somehow outlived Everest Bridge, which some say doesn't really happen much," Jin said weaving his web and prodding the professor.

"It's kind of old news, Jin and I really don't have much time in the midst of all these preparations for next week."

"No problem, Doc," Jin said, closing up his backpack as he stood up to go, "I guess I just thought that an esteemed college professor of film at one of the top schools in the nation would want first dibs on a story that's so ridiculous yet so utterly convincing that this "corruptor of the youth" is going to get a chance to befuddle an educated audience of professors and some of the brightest and budding minds of tomorrow with his ideas."

Jin paused for effect, letting his propaganda flurry settle to the ground and sink in before releasing his atomic bomb. "Not sure why but I just thought you'd want to check it out for yourself before I pass this footage off to the highest bidding news teams who initially ran stories on Deavensby months ago. Apparently they must have thought that this myth of a man would be too much of a vegetable for the rest of his life that they didn't even think to follow up with this totally rare phenomenon to see if the same wizardry that protected him from death might also be able to magically grant him a new life worth living."

Jin continued, "Imagine their reactions when they see footage of their own hometown heroes/university students who pulled this disastrous man out of the river, now bonding with the psycho-spiritual suicide survivor. As if that wasn't enough of a happy ending, this mythical phoenix is now scheduled to give a touching message on the human mental capacity to overcome any obstacles including death itself in order to rise to new levels of happiness."

"Geez Jin, you never mentioned that you had footage!"

Jin shrugged and said, "Straight from the horse's mouth."

Donovan responded again, "No one could ever say that you don't talk a good game, Jin. Maybe you should be pitching a speech at the conference as well."

"Can you get me a spot?" Jin said facetiously with a triumphant smile.

"Alright buddy let's have a look at that footage," Professor Donovan conceded.

After watching the video Professor Donovan stroked his beard and said, "Now I know why you came to me first instead of heading straight to local broadcasting. As I mentioned before, your pitch is perfect, and you talk a good game, but your footage needs some serious maintenance."

To this Jin acknowledged temporary defeat with a knowing grin before Donovan advanced, "If you don't knock it out of the park, you'll never make it to first base with any of these local stations. Here's what I'm going to do for you to make sure you hit a grand slam, Jin. You let me put my name on this project with you and I'll professionally edit it from scratch using strong commentary to delete the garbage scenes and amplify it up to the high production quality that you need. I assure you that I can not only get this into the right hands, but that it will be broadcasted through local media on the morning of the conference before the conference even begins. Not only that, but if I know these companies well, and trust me I do, they're going to want to have news crews present for Skyler's Saturday morning speech."

"Now, I'll admit that as outlandish his ideas and as strange and eccentric as this Skyler character is, he has quite the story to tell. He's kind of a freak of nature, but if he can still make his words dance and perform like he did in this video, the news crews will be there to take his story to national news, talk shows and you never know what screens his little dream could reach from there. I've seen more than a few speakers' careers take off after getting a start and developing there wings here on our launch pad."

"However, let me also be clear that if Skyler belly flops and for any reason at all can't deliver, well, I can assure you that these programs in the age of the internet with their smear campaigns, will make Mr. Skyler wish he had never regained consciousness from his encounter with that old Suicide Bridge. Either way though, Jin, your resume and your rap sheet will tower over your competition long before you even walk across the stage if you know what I mean! That's assuming you still choose to finish your education. But I assure you that with a resume like yours will be after I'm done with this video, it won't be necessary. So, what you do you say? Do we have a deal?"

III
THE RIVER OF TEARS

The night before the conference, Skyler had a dream that he was speaking from the stage in the arena to a crowd of people seated on the floor chairs while all of the rest of the seats in the stadium were empty. In real life, Skyler had previously been to the arena for athletic events, but never for a speaking engagement. When he saw all of the chairs on the basketball court in the dream, his nerves were calmed somewhat because even though the floor was covered with seats, the size of the audience didn't seem like much in comparison to what could have been if the seating encircling the whole stadium was filled.

Nevertheless, he still couldn't get beyond the strange and overbearing feeling that the stage and the gymnasium were serious overkill for the day's purposes. In addition, he forgot his notes in the locker room where he'd been prepping himself. Amber was seated on the front row and the theme of overkill that permeated his dream had caused Skyler to interrupt his own speech at various points as he repeatedly covered his microphone to curiously ask Amber, *"Shouldn't a university of this size and reputation have smaller auditoriums and conference rooms for audiences like this one?"* In response, Amber would just smile back at Skyler cordially, and with a shooing hand gesture prompting him to keep speaking, to which Skyler would awkwardly resume his story.

In a second dream that night, camera crews were filming him at Everest Bridge, as Skyler was about to leap, but this time he wasn't leaping to hurt himself. For some strange reason, Skyler was trying to show the world that if he jumped, wings would unfold from his back like the story of Amalie from the book that he was listening to on the day that he quit his job. When he stepped off of the banister, Skyler could feel the weird sensation of wings trying to protrude from just beneath the surface of his skin, but they stubbornly refused to do his bidding. As a result, Skyler struggled frantically against the rushing wind, helplessly realizing this was indeed going to be the end.

As soon as he hit the water, the scenery instantly changed and he found himself sitting at the bottom of the sea in a studio across from famous talk show host, Ailynn Spellings. He was seated on a couch before a crowd just like any late-night show. The only difference was that there was water everywhere. Everyone should have been drowning, but the show went on as if everyone was fine. And almost everyone was fine. Sure, they took in a little water as they inhaled, and bubbles exited their mouths or their nostrils as they exhaled, but no one was bothered by it. No one was bothered by it except for a young man in the third to last row in the back-left corner of the studio.

It started out with a simple little cough in a tiny parade of bubbles that followed just before the host, Ailynn Spellings looked over to Skyler and said, "Some very notable publications have praised your story as a life-changing demonstration of the human capacity, not only to survive but also to thrive when genuine self-help principles touch and collide with the desperate life of a suicide."

Skyler nodded as he heard more coughing from the general direction of the back-left corner.

Ailynn went on, "Others have said that Zenith was not an aspect of your deepest self, but rather just a figment of your imagination."

This was followed by more coughing, only now the coughing was so violent that bubbles had taken over the whole left side of the room so much so that Skyler could not even see the man who was coughing anymore even though he had stopped paying attention to the host as he tried to see if the man was ok.

It struck Skyler that the host and most of the people in the audience were not concerned about the man in the slightest because Spellings was fully focused on Skyler, and the audience kept their eyes fixed on the two of them seated on the stage. Skyler would have thought that their actions seemed mechanical, or even robotic, until he detected that many of them were more annoyed by the disturbance than just unemotionally invested automatons blankly staring ahead. Eventually, although conflicted, Skyler surrendered to the eyes of the crowd and redirected his attention to his host on the stage.

Ailynn continued, "Some have even said that you never even jumped off the bridge in the first place and that it was all just a big hoax."

As she said this, the coughing died down and bubbles dissipated to Skyler's great relief. Skyler looked over again just checking once more to make sure that the man was all right. However, to his horror he found that the only reason that the bubbles had stopped was because the man was now forcefully holding his breath.

Further, it seemed that he was holding his breath so effectively that his face was beginning to turn purple. Nevertheless, all eyes remained fixed on Skyler, and Ailynn Spellings drilled on.

"But regardless of what people have said, whether they loved your story, hated it, believed it, were sympathetic to it, felt apathetic towards it or whether they thought that it was just plain stupid, you and your story of Zenith have swept the world with a dizzying fury. So, I must ask, what do you have to say about all of this, Mr. Skyler Deavensby?" She said this in a repulsed and demeaning tone as if she was a high school principal, wrinkling her nose while questioning and threatening a student for planting stink bombs throughout the school.

Skyler felt stuck to his seat. He really wanted to answer the host's questions, but he had an even greater desire to help the young man in the back who was now suffocating himself because he couldn't breathe underwater. Emotionally torn between the pressure of the crowd and Ailynn Spellings on one side and the turmoil and plight of the young man dying because Skyler was too paralyzed to do anything, Skyler screamed out, *"Somebody help!"* As he said this, he awoke from his dream with a jolt and found himself drenched in a puddle of cold sweat. He didn't know if he had yelled out loud or just in his dream, but Tulip who was lying next to him still lay there sleeping soundly and breathing evenly.

Looking around, Skyler could see that it was still dark outside, but he couldn't sleep, and he had an uncommon urge to return to Everest Bridge. Ever since he'd come out of his coma, he wanted to go back there for some unexplainable reason, and he knew that he would go there eventually when the time was right. Though it was illogical, he knew that that time had come. Skyler didn't know how he knew that to be true, but he knew that the feeling was undeniable. Maybe it was the pressure of the conference. Maybe it had something to do with his fear of speaking. Surely his odd dreams from the night before had something to do with it. But now was the time. The irresistible pull that drove him to Everest at this time of night was eerie, but he couldn't deny a strange feeling that it was also unavoidable.

In Skyler's experience the more irresistible his desire to do something, the more irrational he became towards it, for better or worse. He knew what Tulip would say and he knew what she would do if he told her where he was going. She'd say this was an awful idea especially now that he was doing so well for himself and was beginning to generate some positive momentum towards building a new life. She'd say this was impulsive and irresponsible. Then she'd try to dissuade him. When that didn't work, she'd simply say that she was going with him. That's why she didn't need to know. He needed to go this one alone. What was the worst that could happen anyway? He wasn't sure what he'd find at the bridge. He didn't even know what he was looking for if anything at all. All he knew was that he had to do this, and he had to do it right now.

Steeling himself with resolve, Skyler quietly got up out of bed and got himself ready for the big day. Amber had called Skyler three days in advance to let him know that the conference schedule had been rearranged and that he would be the first to speak. Skyler was cool with that because he'd rather not wait to hear all of the other seasoned speakers, knowing that he wouldn't be able to avoid comparing their presentations to the material that he had prepared, shamefully. In his eyes, it was better for him to just get it over with anyway so that he wouldn't have to deal with his nerves all throughout the day. With this in mind, he wrote a note to Tulip and the kids saying,

> *Good morning lovelies, I got up at the crack of dawn to do some soul searching and last-minute preparations for my talk. I'll meet you all at the conference this morning since I have to arrive early for sound check. Wish me luck . . . Thanks for being*

*the roots that keep me stretching to the sky. I couldn't
do any of this without you.*

I love you

Dad

When he arrived at the outskirts of the bridge, although it was
not visible, the low-lying sun had just begun to comb a sliver of
the sky with its morning rays like a sleepy old man groping his
bedroom walls in search of the light switch. The effect was blue,
orange, red and purple hues just barely beginning to touch a thin
jet stream of clouds. In a flash, Skyler realized that if he quickened
his pace to the middle of the bridge, he just might be able to catch
the sunrise on the horizon as it regained its eternal youth after
being swallowed up by its sole nemesis, the night sky. Arriving at
the high point, Skyler was satisfied to see that he'd made it with a
few minutes left to spare even though he was still internally torn
and exhausted from his journey and the previous night's dreams
that still haunted him.

The truth was that the path to the bridge had its own
emotional texture and walking along that path instantly wove and
threaded Skyler's thoughts into its familiar designs and patterns
while blanketing him with some of the original feelings that he felt
from the first time that he'd traversed this route. He was
unexpectedly overshadowed by the grip of his trip to the
monstrous bridge and he was beginning to doubt whether coming
was indeed the right decision. Nevertheless, he was here now, in
the belly of the beast and whether it spit him out on dry land or
not, he would ride it for all it was worth.

Looking to the right of him, Skyler saw where the great river
over which he stood banked up against the land that held the

airport. As his eyes continued to scan in that direction, he observed the university arena where he'd be speaking that morning, the shops on the boardwalk strip and finally the ocean just beyond all of it. He sighed in anticipation wondering if he was actually ready for all of this. In order to continue to journey in that direction it would take the courage of self-exposure, self-mastery and self-love.

To his left, Skyler could see the whole town on the plateau from which he had just traveled. He felt a sharp pang of alienation, misfortune and separation as he observed the path of his past, and his eyes retraced his steps back to the supposed coffee shop, the bar, the street where he fell in front of the bus and just beyond the town to the more wooded area where he wrote that miserable goodbye letter to his family over six months ago. When he left the house on the morning of the conference, he'd hoped that a second pilgrimage to the bridge would be inspirational and redemptive; an uplifting review of how far he'd come since his downward spiral. But this journey to the bridge was far from uplifting.

The street where he fell in front of the bus was empty and the bar just around the corner was closed. Of course, he didn't expect to see and strike up a conversation with the bus driver, the rollerblader with the dogs nor the bartender. He just thought that these important places of significance that held indelible memories in his mind would have the power to elicit strong emotion and a sense of prideful triumph over them. It was like he came down here to deliver a knock out blow to these places while boasting that he had won, and they had no power to defeat him. But they just sat there, turned the other cheek, and this mysteriously gave them the upper hand in a strange way. Their silence hit him with a stunning jab between the eyes, unnerved him and left him confused. This trip was supposed to make him feel like a winner running his victory lap where he flaunted his belt as the undisputed champion of a rival that never loses. When those feelings refused to come, he just felt petty, small, insignificant and low.

For months he had fought tooth and nail in order to stay focused on that quite miraculous perspective of this narrative in which all that really mattered was that he was still alive and that he had a second chance. Now his early morning journey had deluded his defenses, sneaking beyond the gate guard of his mind while reminding him that no matter how much he blinded himself to other perspectives, they still had their own crippling validity. Further, these valid perspectives still had the power to see him and maim him if he wasn't careful.

The bridge had never picked a fight with him, nor been his enemy in any way. The simple reality was that Skyler had tried to take his own life and he had failed. And now he was supposed to just confidently walk into a world of academics with future scholars and thought leaders and speak to them with a straight face about how he had been internally fighting and destroying himself but was all better now? Zenith had put a nice band-aid on it and Skyler's mind was completely fixed? Was this really the angle that he was shooting for? And everyone was just supposed to believe him? The host in the dream last night wasn't buying it and she alluded to the fact that others wouldn't either. And why would they? He'd be lucky if they actually let him finish his talk without laughing him off of the stage. Maybe last night's dream was protecting him by warning him to not go through with any of this nonsense. The whole thing just seemed so immature and stupid now. Forget about what Amber thought when she invited him to do this, did he really think this would fly?

Somewhere within him, Skyler knew this line of reasoning was incredibly bi-polar, but he had already snorted it and didn't know how to turn it off. It reminded him of that time as a kid that his parents had opted for him to have laughing gas in order to undergo dental work. However, it was a bad high and Skyler had lost all control of his faculties. All Skyler wanted was for the dentist to *"Turn it off!"* He yelled this line repeatedly and belligerently to no avail through opposing bouts of laughter. Then Skyler lost it and it had gotten so bad that they had to bring in Skyler's dad to hold him down because Skyler had ultimately tried to fight the dentist. All he wanted now was to turn it all off.

It was all so overwhelming that Skyler dropped his head and sighed another deep breath beneath the weight of it all. This was the first time that he had let himself feel the feelings of his old life and his old self. Looking down, he observed that below him was ground zero; the lowest point of his life. It was his ultimate declaration of self-hatred but also the portal through which he had almost escaped from all of the pressure, uncertainty and problems in his life. Even now, the allure had an enticing edge that, just considering for a second, gave him an unexplainable rush of emotion that he could neither deny nor justify. It was that enticing edge that called to his consciousness like a cutter who is irresistibly drawn to the desire of the swift sliding blade that would crawl across her skin in rapid succession regardless of how the pain of destruction will later haunt her when she is in her right mind.

In the midst of all this, he closed his eyes and a thousand treacherous thoughts encircled his head, taunting him. The thoughts flew in flight patterns as if he was their prey or worse just some road kill that they could swoop in to devour and carry off at any moment after a clear break in traffic. However, another peculiar thought, which was not as dark as the rest, flew in just then and perched on Skyler's mind. This one thought came in as naturally as if it was with a whole flock of morning gulls landing on the bridge and claiming their rightful spot as they had done daily since the construction of the bridge. Just because there was a little road kill today didn't negate the fact that this was their morning spot to shoot the breezed and their table on which they conducted their morning routine and squawked their daily business.

Though the darker thoughts had already begun marking their territory by shitting all over Skyler's mind, this new thought had a more recent and consistently staked claim with the owner. This one amiable little thought perched and settled in, which was somehow enough to drive away a thousand darker thoughts convincing them all to go find another bridge, another diner, another mind, another table, another man. The thought that came and cawed a warning command was incomprehensible to the others, but it was a distinct and forceful clarion call awakening the mind of its master.

The command crowned Skyler's bowed head and sinking thoughts with a few words that simply said, *"I'm always safe, always protected, always courageous and always fearless."* This one thought softly and silently reverberated repetitively louder and louder through his whole being until a lovely morning calm settled on Skyler like the rays of the sunrise driving the night from the face of the earth. The construction of these simple short phrases gripped Skyler and shook him awake while shoring up the wobbly integrity of his mental architecture.

When he opened his eyes and lifted his head, everything was brighter as the sun had just begun dawning, yawning and rising in the darkness while turning on the morning. To his further astonishment he saw a vision of people everywhere. Skyler felt as if he was looking out over a sea of people and every ripple on the water below was another beautiful face. There were thousands and even millions of them. The faces peered at him expectantly, but he found that they didn't make him nervous and he didn't shy away or intentionally banish the vision from his mind by closing his eyes or by batting his eyes and blinking it away.

He simply stood there taking it all in and embracing the moment for all it was worth. He saw himself in each face and felt a distinct feeling of oneness that was indescribable to him, but not unfamiliar. He had no idea what his vision meant, but he didn't feel as though he needed to know just then. All he knew was that it felt right, it felt good, he'd found the off switch to banish that terrifying episode of fear and anxiety from his mind and he felt as though he had been screwed in to the energy of the universe.

Ever since he was young, he always felt that he was meant to do something extraordinary with his life and his voice. The problem was, he had spent so much time negating himself that he had succeeded in believing that he had nothing to offer and nothing to share. It was all quite convincing. But he didn't care anymore. If his story was stupid, that was none of his business. Never again would his business be to critique his story. His business was quite simply to share it with any and every person who was interested in hearing it. He was meant to do something extraordinary with his life, but he would do it by simply showing up and being his ordinary self—nothing more, nothing less and no one to impress.

Now as he stood there on the bridge giving and receiving energy to and from the people before him, there was a congruence that registered in him as that familiar feeling of wanting to live into his largeness that he had always desired, yet for years he had simultaneously pushed away. However, something was different in him here. He was no longer a magnet strangely and mysteriously repelling its identical twin and other kin magnets. He was calm, collected, open and connected with this previously estranged part of himself.

This sea of faces, though exponentially larger than any crowd he could ever conceive of himself standing before, was not bigger than him. It was one with him. He stood upright yet comfortable and relaxed, dignified, poised, fully dedicated to and utterly unified with every person that he saw on the ripples of the water. He felt unwaveringly dedicated and set to serve them by simply being present to help others with the transparency of his story and to give his everything to all that was before him.

In his dream from last night he had been trying to prove to the world through the camera crews, that he could fly when all he needed to do was help the one person who was drowning beneath the water. He couldn't fly like Amalie who'd sprouted wings in the story that he had last read on that dreadful day. But the phenomenal news was that he didn't need to. All he had to do was help the people that he could help, beginning with himself. He had painfully discovered that morning that even after all of the positive strides he'd made to keep a strong mind, if he didn't continue to care for himself, he could go from thriving to drowning in an instant. Although his mental episode or little hiccup from this morning had only lasted a few minutes, it was enough to expose him to some hidden dangers within himself of which he had previously been unaware. With this in mind, he vowed to himself that he would live to protect his happiness and his mental well-being at all costs.

Even though he had been self-conscious about speaking publicly, now Skyler could see that it didn't matter that he wasn't the most polished speaker. It dawned on him that he didn't have any notes or organized outlines when he spoke to the students in the hospital, so it couldn't have been that he was being invited there because his story was so polished. Rather, he was being invited there because of his story's power. It wasn't the *intelligent* nature of his story, but its *intuitive* nature that registered with his listeners at a deep level and made them confident that his story could also help others.

Further, it didn't matter what people said and thought about him nor his story of Zenith. All he had to do was wake up and embody the truth of what his deepest self had yelled and screamed in his dream when he'd said, *"Somebody help!"* Skyler recognized now that he was both the drowning man who needed help in his dream and the "somebody" who could "help". Knowing this, he made a second vow that day that no matter what happened in the arena this morning nor how people responded to his story from now on, he would concern himself with nothing other than serving those who needed him most in every possible way that he could.

Now he clearly understood the words of Lao Tzu that said, "All streams flow to the sea because it is lower than they are. Humility gives it its power. If you want to govern the people, you must put yourself below them. If you want to lead the people, you must learn how to follow them."[84] Just as humility gave the sea it's power to stay connected to every mountain stream, transparency would give Skyler his power to share his story and connect to those who really needed him most. Everything was clear now. He would teach his story with his voice; he would write it in his own autobiographical story and he would screen write it. He would mentor others just as he had mentored Amber, Bryan and Micah when they had come to him seeking a better understanding.

Finally, he'd build an organization dedicated to suicide prevention, mental wellbeing and dream building.

As for what he truly thought of himself, regardless of what any naysayers might have thought, he didn't actually believe that his story was stupid. He thought that it was "bonkers", "intense" and "badass" as his newfound friends would say. Skyler smiled for a minute as he remembered the students' mutual excitement at everything that he had shared with them and he wondered how many of them might be there for his little talk that morning. Something ominous about the moment reminded Skyler of Zenith. So, he paused temporarily before stepping off towards his destination and took one last look out over the water, wondering if she was still tucked away somewhere down there amid the multitude of all the beautiful faces.

MORE TO DISCOVER

Mirrors Of The Sun
Finding Reflections Of Light In The Shittiness Of Life

Sleeping With Enormity
The Art Of Seducing Your Dreams & Living With Passion

Giants At Play
Finding Wisdom, Courage, & Acceptance To Encounter Your
Destiny

CONNECT WITH CURTIS

Email:
radiatenewrealities@gmail.com

NOTES

[1] James Hollis, Finding Meaning in the Second Half of Life (New York: Penguin Group, Inc.).

[2] Henry David Thoreau, Walden (New York: Thomas Y. Crowell & Company) 8.

[3] Plato, Apology (London: Harvard University Press) 38A.

[4] Claude M. Bristol, TNT: It Rocks the Earth (Midwest Journal Press) 26.

[5] Richard Rohr, Falling Upward: A Spirituality for the Two Halves of Life (San Francisco: Jossey-Bass A Wiley Imprint).

[6] C.S. Lewis, Mere Christianity (New York: Harper Collins Publishers) 216.

[7] Friedrich Nietzsche, Thus Spoke Zarathustra (New York: Penguin Group) 69.

[8] Friedrich Nietzsche, Thus Spoke Zarathustra (New York: Penguin Group) 54-56.

[9] Rumi, The Pocket Rumi (Boston: Shambhala Publications, Inc.) 144.

[10] Law of Attraction Explained with Denzel Washington, Will Smith & Other Stars: Goodchild (Channel). https://www.youtube.com/watch?v=4SpJlqs4PT0

[11] Motivation - The Key to Accomplishments by Zig Ziglar. https://music.apple.com/us/album/motivation-the-key-to-accomplishments/335522097

[12] Dan Millman, Way of the Peaceful Warrior: A Book That Changes Lives (Tiburon: HJ Kramer Inc. & New World Library) 105.

[13] Eckhart Tolle, The Power of Now (Novato: Namaste Publishing and New World Library) 218.

[14] Henriette Anne Klauser, Write It Down, Make It Happen: Knowing What You Want And Getting it! (New York: Simon & Schuster).

[15] Rhonda Byrne, The Secret (New York: Simon & Schuster) 95-98.

[16] Rhonda Byrne, The Magic (New York: Atria Books of Simon & Schuster).

[17] Law of Attraction Explained with Denzel Washington, Will Smith & Other Stars: Goodchild (Channel). https://www.youtube.com/watch?v=4SpJlqs4PT0

[18] Wallace D. Wattles, The Science of Getting Rich (Natrona Heights: General Press).

[19] Neville Goddard, The Power of Awareness (Natrona Heights: General Press).

[20] Henriette Anne Klauser, Write It Down, Make It Happen: Knowing What You Want and Getting It! (New York: Simon & Schuster).

[21] Mel Robbins, The 5 Second Rule: Transform Your Life, Work and Confidence with Everyday Courage (United States: Savio Republic).

[22] Eckhart Tolle, The Power of Now (Novato: Namaste Publishing and New World Library) 3-5.

[23] Robert Greene, Mastery (New York: Viking Penguin) 40-42.

[24] Benedict Carey, Expert on Mental Illness Reveals Her Own Fight (Article): https://www.nytimes.com/2011/06/23/health/23lives.html

[25] Widely attributed to Fyodor Dostoyevsky.

[26] Benedict Carey, Expert on Mental Illness Reveals Her Own Fight (Article): https://www.nytimes.com/2011/06/23/health/23lives.html

[27] Zig Ziglar. See You at the Top (Gretna: Pelican Publishing Company) 164.

[28] Zig Ziglar. See You at the Top (Gretna: Pelican Publishing Company) 45.

[29] Marcus Aurelius, Meditations (New York: Random House) 37-38.

[30] Shel Silverstein, Where the Sidewalk Ends (New York: Harper Collins Children's Books) 27.

[31] Napoleon Hill, Laws of Success Full Length: Love.Inspires.Faith.Empowers (Channel). https://www.youtube.com/watch?v=8EQWhQt9OQo

[32] Napoleon Hill, Laws of Success Full Length: Love.Inspires.Faith.Empowers (Channel). https://www.youtube.com/watch?v=8EQWhQt9OQo

[33] Widely attributed to Henry Ford

[34] Napoleon Hill, Laws of Success Full Length: Love.Inspires.Faith.Empowers (Channel). https://www.youtube.com/watch?v=8EQWhQt9OQo

[35] Paulo Coelho, The Alchemist (New York: Harper Collins Publishers).

[36] Frank McCourt, Angela's Ashes (New York, Scribner, Simon & Schuster Inc.) 208.

[37] Florence Scovel Shin, The Game of Life and How to Play It (Oregan Publishing).

[38] Russell H. Conwell, Acres of Diamonds. (New York: Harper & Brothers Publishers) 4.

[39] Russell H. Conwell, Acres of Diamonds. (New York: Harper & Brothers Publishers) 5.

[40] Russell H. Conwell, Acres of Diamonds. (New York: Harper & Brothers Publishers) 8.

[41] Unknown.

[42] Rumi, Unknown.

[43] Lao Tzu, Tao Te Ching: A New English Version By Stephen Mitchell (New York: Harper Collins Publishers) 11.

[44] Byron Katie, Loving What Is: Four Questions That Can Change Your Life (New York: Harmony Books) 87.

[45] Paulo Coelho, The Alchemist (New York: Harper Collins Publishers).

[46] Unknown.

[47] Howard Thurman, Unknown.

[48] Joseph Campbell, A Joseph Campell Companion: Reflections On the Art of Living (San Anselmo: Joseph Campbell Foundation).

[49] Florence Scovel Shin. The Game of Life and How to Play It (Oregan Publishing).

[50] African Proverb, Anonymous.

[51] James Hollis, The Middle Passage: From Misery to Meaning In Midlife (Toronto: Inner City Books) 7.

[52] Pam Grout, E-Cubed: 9 More Energy Experiments That Prove Manifesting Magic and Miracles is Your Full-Time Gig (Carlsbad: Hay House).

[53] Eckhart Tolle, The Power of Now (Novato: Namaste Publishing and New World Library) 11.

[54] Soren Kierkegaard, The Sickness Unto Death (New York: Penguin Books) 69.

[55] Paulo Coelho, The Alchemist (New York: Harper Collins Publishers).

[56] Paulo Coelho, The Alchemist (New York: Harper Collins Publishers).

[57] Bertice Berry, "Home" (Website). http://www.berticeberrynow.com/home.html

[58] Oprah Winfrey, Super Soul – EP.#10: Paulo Coelho, Part 1: What If the Universe Conspired in Your Favor?: Super Soul Podcast (Channel). https://youtu.be/sVQzNr8ACtY

[59] Joseph Campbell, Pathways to Bliss: Mythology and Personal Transformation (Novato: New World Library) xxiv.

[60] Pam Grout, Thank & Grow Rich: A 30 Day Experiment in Shameless Gratitude and Unabashed Joy (Carlsbad: Hay House).

[61] Neville Goddard, Believe It In (Marquette: LGT Digital, Audio) 15:45.

[62] Widely Attributed to Jim Kwik.

[63] Oxford Dictionary of English, "Definition of Intuition in English by Lexico Dictionaries" (Website). https://www.lexico.com/en/definition/intuition

[64] Oxford Dictionary of English, "Definition of Intuition in English by Lexico Dictionaries" (Website). https://www.lexico.com/en/definition/intuition

[65] Hafiz, I Heard God Laughing: Poems of Hope and Joy: Renderings of Hafiz by Daniel Ladinsky (New York: Penguin Books) 36.

[66] The Neville Goddard Lectures: Vol 4 (Altenmunster, Germany: Jazzybee Verlag).

[67] Neville Goddard, The Power of Awareness (Natrona Heights: General Press).

[68] Neville Goddard, The Power of Awareness (Natrona Heights: General Press).

[69] George Bernard Shaw, Man and Superman: A Comedy and a Philosophy (New York: Brentano's) 238.

[70] Neville Goddard, The Power of Awareness (Natrona Heights: General Press).

[71] Neville Goddard, Feeling is the Secret: The Art of Realizing Your Desire (Natrona Heights: General Press).

[72] Genevieve Davis, Becoming Magic: A Course In Manifesting An Exceptional Life: Book 1 (Self Published: Amazon Digital Services, LLC).

[73] Florence Scovel Shinn, Your Word Is Your Wand (Musaicum Books).

[74] Lil Wayne, The Carter IV Album: Nightmares of the Bottom (Young Money Entertainment).

[75] Esther Hicks, Ask and It Is Given: Learning to Manifest Your Desires (Carlsbad: Hay House, Inc).

[76] Neville Goddard, Out of This World: Audio Edition (New York: Gildan Media, LLC) 53:40.

[77] Lao Tzu, Tao Te Ching: A New English Version by Stephen Mitchell (New York: Harper Collins Publishers).

[78] Lao Tzu, Tao Te Ching: A New English Version by Stephen Mitchell (New York: Harper Collins Publishers).

[79] Lao Tzu, Tao Te Ching: A New English Version by Stephen Mitchell (New York: Harper Collins Publishers).

[80] Lao Tzu, Tao Te Ching: A New English Version by Stephen Mitchell (New York: Harper Collins Publishers).

[81] Ayn Rand, Atlas Shrugged (New York: Penguin Books) 1069.

[82] Unknown.

[83] Hafiz, I Heard God Laughing: Poems of Hope and Joy: Renderings of Hafiz by Daniel Ladinsky (New York: Penguin Books) 7.

[84] Lao Tzu, Tao Te Ching: A New English Version by Stephen Mitchell (New York: Harper Collins Publishers).